A Destroyed Love

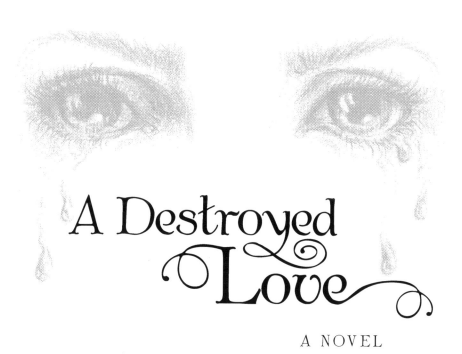

A Destroyed Love

A NOVEL

GINNY ROBERTS

ARCHWAY
PUBLISHING

Archway Publishing books may be ordered through booksellers or by contacting:

Archway Publishing
1663 Liberty Drive
Bloomington, IN 47403
www.archwaypublishing.com
1 (888) 242-5904

ISBN: 978-1-4808-6996-7 (sc)
ISBN: 978-1-4808-6997-4 (hc)
ISBN: 978-1-4808-6995-0 (e)

Library of Congress Control Number: 2018966378

Print information available on the last page.

Archway Publishing rev. date: 12/14/2018

Dedicated to

Gracie,

my thirteen-year-old silky terrier, who
suffered many days without adequate
affection while the book was in progress

Acknowledgments

Special thanks to Debra Creech, my lifelong friend, who encouraged me to keep writing when my life got in the way and I was ready to give up, gave me ideas when I drew a blank, and provided her editing expertise. Debra drew the cover artwork as well. Thanks to Anne MacLeod for editing the manuscript and giving me excellent suggestions on how to move the story along. Thank you to Andrea Hagner, who read the manuscript and gave me valuable suggestions. Lastly, thanks to my husband, Ed, who spent many hours encouraging me to continue working on the book and provided his word processing expertise. Without the help of these people, you wouldn't be reading the book.

Chapter 1

ood morning!" the voice on the clock radio blared. "Love is in the air today—it's Valentine's Day, the most romantic day of the year. This is your Z103 host, David, and I'll be here all morning, taking love song requests for that special person in your life."

As I was awakened by the DJ's greeting, I pulled the covers up over my head and thought, *Good grief. I'm going to have to listen to this all day.* I knew that Valentine's Day meant people would be coming into my interior design shop looking for unique gifts and talking about their plans for the evening. I could feel the pain welling up in my heart. *Oh no*, I said to myself. *You are not going to be sad today.* I threw back the covers and forced myself out of bed. After a long, soothing shower, with coffee cup in hand, I deliberately chose a black sheath dress and pinned my blonde hair back into a tight bun to erase any softness. As I reached for my earrings, I hesitated over the small diamond-encrusted ruby hearts that had been last year's Valentine's present from Ray. *No! No hearts—not today.*

On the short walk from my townhouse to my shop across the street, I passed people with happy faces, and each smile made me struggle to control my emotions. While I unlocked the shop door, my two young employees, Ellen and Janet, arrived right behind me. As we hung up our coats, I said, "You look lovely in your red dresses and heart earrings, ladies. Today should be a fun workday for you. I have some projects and prep work to do for my buying trip to New York tomorrow, so I'll be working in my office all day."

Out of sight in my studio, I could still hear occasional laughter and excited talk, but my tasks kept me engrossed.

Finally, the workday was over, and we bundled ourselves into our coats and closed the shop. Ellen and Janet hurried away to meet their dates, and I headed home.

I arrived home chilled from my short walk on that freezing day, with my fingers and toes feeling like blocks of ice. I turned on my fireplace's gas logs and sat down on the sofa to warm up. As I gazed into the flames, I became so overwhelmed with memories that I briefly gave in to my sorrow. Last Valentine's Day, I had been snuggling in front of a fire like that one with my beloved Ray, drinking a bottle of wine from his collection, eating red velvet cake, and planning our future together.

When I heard my grandfather clock strike seven, I quickly came to my senses and remembered my vow that I was never going to fall in love again. I wasn't going to go through heartache like that again. *Stop this, Christina! You're doing just fine by yourself. Love hurts too much, so forget about it.*

Wiping the tears away from my cheeks, I decided to make myself a real sit-down dinner. I still had a bottle of the same kind of wine Ray and I had shared last Valentine's Day, so I thought, *I'll start with a glass of wine.* Just as I picked up the wine opener, someone knocked on my door. When I answered, my friend Faye stood there with a bottle of wine in her hands. She said, "I didn't want you to be alone this evening."

"Please come in," I said. "You're just in time to have Valentine's dinner with me. But first, let's get that wine open."

Later, while we sipped our after-dinner glass of wine, Faye said, "Christina, do you realize we have been close friends ever since we met when our ex-husbands were college roommates? We were even bridesmaids in each other's weddings. Now we're both divorcées. How did we end up like this?"

"Gosh, Faye," I responded. "I have no idea how we misjudged our exes that badly. When I said, 'Until death do us part,' I thought my life would be only with him."

"Me too," said Faye. "Well, let's not waste any more of our evening thinking about them. After this good meal, we must cut that delicious-looking red velvet cake. When it comes to knowing how to fix a meal, you never forget a thing."

While eating our cake with ice cream on the side, we watched a funny Hallmark TV movie.

As the evening came to a close, Faye gathered her purse to leave.

"Thanks for thinking of me this evening," I said.

By the time I'd finished doing a few chores and packing for my trip the following day, it was bedtime. As I settled down to sleep, I thought about when I had met Ray seven years ago.

After graduating from Parsons School of Design in New York City, I got married and went to work for an upscale furniture store in Williamsburg, Virginia. Ray came into the store one day, and I helped him select furniture for his home. Although I was impressed with his distinguished look and assured manner, I thought of him only as a client. A few years later, when my husband and I divorced, I decided it was the perfect time to make my dream of having my own interior design business a reality. In my search to find a store location, I was pleasantly surprised to discover that the well-dressed owner of a prominent commercial real estate office was my former client, Raymond Hatsell.

Ray helped me find a space in a small shopping strip he owned in Williamsburg and was instrumental in easing the way for me to renovate it. He would occasionally stop in during the remodeling to see the progress. Late one evening, he said, "Christina, I bet you haven't had dinner yet, have you?"

"You're right, Ray. I haven't. I've been too busy to even think about eating."

"Since we both need to eat, come with me."

"Okay, let me get my coat," I said. "I'm famished."

Over the next few months, Ray used his expertise as an established businessman to help me learn the responsibilities and hard work involved in starting a business from scratch. He encouraged and complimented me. He wanted me to succeed and was happy for me when I made progress toward success. As he became closer as a friend, he was kind and protective of me as I healed from the wounds of my ruined marriage and grew into a confident, independent woman. As weeks turned into months and then into years, Ray was first my mentor, then my best friend, and finally my lover.

I was somewhat in awe of the high society in which I found myself. Ray was proud to have me on his arm as he introduced me to important and influential people in his world of community events, country club happenings, and lavish parties. I learned the art of home entertaining by being his hostess for events at his large, beautiful home, which overlooked the James River. He eventually convinced me to move in with him, and I learned to work with a house staff as efficiently as I did with Ellen and Janet. When my business was a financial success after the completion of my five-year plan, I happily agreed to marry him and began to plan our wedding day.

Our relationship was warm and comfortable. I followed Ray's example of keeping my nights free of work, so we had dinner together every night and talked about our workdays. Ray always laughed at the gossip I heard from my clients and customers. When we ate at home, I loved that he shared a glass of wine with me in the kitchen while we worked together to prepare our meals. He enjoyed introducing me to his favorite wines that he kept in his impressive basement wine cellar. Some of our favorite getaway weekends were for wine-tasting festivals.

Sadly, I thought of the day Ray died. We were at a fall wine-tasting festival in western Virginia, when he suddenly had difficulty breathing and then collapsed to the ground. When the paramedics arrived, they tried everything to revive him, but nothing worked. Now, a little more than a year later, his death was still unbelievable, and the thought that I would have to live the rest of my life without him was unbearable.

Sometimes, though, I felt strongly that he was still with me. On that Valentine's night, as I dreamily lay in my warm bed, I could all but feel him lying beside me. I smiled, knowing I had had the kind of love with him that most people never had. There would never be anyone else who could compare to Ray.

Chapter 2

Leaving on my annual buying trip to New York City the next morning was a bittersweet event for me since it was the first one I had gone on without Ray. While planning the trip, I had been able to keep my sadness under control, but as soon as I boarded the plane and took my seat, thoughts of our past trips flooded back into my mind. We always had made an exciting weekend of it, staying in a luxury hotel and going to a Broadway play. We'd especially enjoyed our walks down the sidewalks past the major department stores, admiring their window displays and discussing how I could adapt them for my shop.

I knew Ray would not want me to be sad, so I gave myself a mental shake and concentrated on my upcoming visit with my vendor, Holly, who was an old classmate and good friend from Parsons. She always had great ideas and did incredible design work, so I couldn't wait to see her new home-accessory collection.

When the plane landed at LaGuardia Airport, I felt the thrill of being back in the city, marveling that so many people could live and work there. I thought about how wonderful it had been to go to college there in the most exciting city in the world. In the cab, I spent the whole trip to Holly's townhouse in Greenwich Village looking up at the impossibly high skyscrapers and down at the throngs of people trying to maneuver through and around each other on the sidewalks. The jerky movements of the cab as we navigated through the noisy traffic congestion made me suddenly thankful for the slower pace of my home in Virginia.

I told the driver to let me out at Washington Square Park, which was near Holly's home. The February air was cold and crisp as I walked past Washington Square Arch and smiled at several teenagers who were no doubt NYU students on their way to class. My smart burgundy wool suit, fitted camel overcoat, and small overnight bag were in sharp contrast to their mile-long scarves, oversize black sweaters, ragged jeans, and large portfolios. I felt a penetrating pang of nostalgia. *Oh, to be young and intense again.* It seemed a long time ago since I had been that happy yet so serious, when the most important thing in the world had been to get a project handed in on time. How many times had I stayed up all night working, only to start all over again the next day on the next project? It was another lifetime ago now.

Leaving the park, I glanced at my watch and was pleased to see that I would be right on time for my appointment with Holly. Two blocks later, I was ringing the doorbell of my friend's brownstone and then swept into her hug.

"Christina! How wonderful to see you, and how cold you look! Come in! Let's get you warmed up." Holly hung my coat in the antique armoire she used as a closet and hustled me down the hallway to the kitchen. As always, we were as comfortable together as if we had just seen each other yesterday instead of last year. Despite our similar personalities, we had always been opposites in looks and style. I was slim, my long blonde hair was straight and shiny, and my clothing style was classic. On the other hand, Holly's curly dark hair and hand-painted shirts in extravagant colors left no doubt she was an artist, and I couldn't wait to see the unusual items she had created since my last visit. After sharing a pot of hot Earl Grey tea, we went to Holly's studio, where I spent several hours picking out stock to be shipped back to my shop. I loved some accessories so much that they went immediately into a box to be checked in for my flight home. Then

I saw it: a small wooden statue of a quirky little man holding a bottle of wine. I was immediately attached to it and could see Ray holding the wine bottle.

Holly had a big smile on her face when I asked her, "Did you design this statue for me?"

"Yes," she said, "it's my gift to you to honor Ray."

I gave her a warm thank-you embrace and said, "I'll always cherish this. I know exactly where I'll put it in the shop. It'll be in a place of honor on the shelf behind my counter, where I can smile at it every day." Holly carefully wrapped it so I could carry it on board instead of checking it or shipping it with the rest of my order.

With my shopping and packing finished, we were free to go out to dinner and do more catching up. Because of Ray's death, Holly had insisted I stay with her instead of going to a lonely hotel room. Back in the brownstone after dinner, we relaxed with wine and laughed as I told Holly all about how friends were trying to fix me up with men. Sometimes they tricked me by inviting me to dinner with them along with a single guy friend. They kept hoping I would change my mind about never getting involved with a man again.

As our laughter wound down, our mood turned a little more somber. Both of us had had early marriages that burned out quickly. Afterward, we both had concentrated on our careers with much success. Holly was still enjoying her work, surrounded as she was by the energy of her many creative friends, but I was submerging into what was now a one-person show. Over the years of working with Ray to build up my business, we had become a loving couple. Now that he was gone, I missed both his physical presence and the mundane day-to-day life we'd had, and I occasionally yearned to be part of a couple again. To my shock, I had even caught myself wondering if I would ever have a family of my own. Looking at Holly with wide eyes, I suddenly realized I needed to get those thoughts out of my head, reminding myself that to love someone, I had to be open to the possibility of being hurt. My grief from losing Ray was still so overpowering that I never wanted to experience that pain again.

"Ah," said Holly, noticing the teary brightness of my eyes. "The wine's talking—it's telling us to go to bed." She showed me to the guest room, which she had warmly decorated with her own drawings and textiles.

My trip back home early the next morning was uneventful. I sent the carton of smaller accessories on through check-in and carefully carried the box with my wooden sculpture with me and held it on my lap on the plane. During the short trip home, I visualized how I would rearrange the merchandise to show off the new items to their best advantage. As I mentally sifted through my inventory, my eyes were drawn to the brightening sky as the sun rose above the clouds. Then my mind turned to how Ray used to fall asleep with his head on my shoulder while holding my hand. Gradually, my thoughts scattered and then ceased altogether as I relaxed and leaned back in my seat.

Chapter 3

FEBRUARY, YEAR ONE
WILLIAMSBURG, VIRGINIA

When the plane landed at the airport back home, I retrieved my box of accessories from the baggage carousel and slung my overnight bag over my shoulder. With Holly's gift clasped tightly with one arm and the much larger box with the other, I headed to my car. The longer I walked, the bigger and heavier the box seemed to get, until I began to struggle with its weight and bulkiness. Suddenly, it was taken out of my arms, and I gasped in shock.

"Oh, I'm sorry," a deep male voice said. "I didn't mean to scare you. You just looked like you needed a little help."

As our eyes met, I felt a shiver of recognition, although I knew I had never seen him before. In that moment, I took in everything about him—his height, his smile, his close-cut brown hair tinged with gray, his navy blazer and khaki pants— and regained my composure enough to answer. "Thank you so much. I was about two seconds away from dropping it." At the same time, I thought, *What a gentleman, and he's nice looking too.*

He shifted the box to his hip and bowed his head toward me. "May I escort you to your car?"

I happily answered, "Of course. It's just over there."

"Where have you been to come back laden with so many

packages?" he asked as we walked. I briefly told him about my buying trip. In return, he said he was working on a construction project in the area and had flown in to check on it. By that time, we'd reached my car and put my packages inside. My heart beat faster as we stood there smiling at each other. He seemed as taken with me as I was with him. Finally, he glanced over toward a small restaurant just across the narrow road from the parking lot.

"Look, I know I'm a stranger, but would you walk over there and have a cup of coffee with me?"

I was pleased he wanted to continue our conversation, but outwardly, I seemed to deliberate his request before answering. "All right, I can do that."

"Wonderful!" He grinned and held out his hand to shake mine. "My name is Bradford Hightower. Please call me Brad."

"And I'm Christina Larsen."

He tucked my hand into the crook of his arm, and we walked the short distance to the restaurant. As the waitress seated us, she told us we were special customers because the restaurant was going out of business at the end of that workday. Brad and I burst out laughing.

"I'm sorry," he said to the waitress. "That just struck me as funny." He turned to me. "I mean, what are the odds that we would choose a bankrupt business for our first date?"

"Oh, is that what this is?" I replied with a smile.

"You'd better believe it," he answered. "Now, tell me more about your interior design business."

Although I answered his question rationally, I found I was having some trouble with my concentration as I told him about the pressures of owning a successful business. At the same time, I thought, *I can't wait to tell Holly about meeting this guy at the airport. She isn't going to believe me.*

"Yes, yes, I know what you mean," he responded passionately. "I'm the owner of a business too." He went on to tell me how he had taken a small one-horse construction business and made it into a large company that did jobs for the government as well as for individuals and corporations. "It has grown to the point now that I have projects that keep me hopping all over several states. The central business office is located near Charlottesville, and I live just outside of Lynchburg," he told me. "But since I have a plane, I can go anywhere at any time. And that gives me an excuse to fly, which is my favorite thing to do." He looked down at his hands curled around his coffee cup and then up at me. "Neither of us is wearing a ring. I'm divorced. Are you?" At my nod, he said, "Well, that's that. When will I see you again?"

Although his take-charge attitude was oddly thrilling, my natural caution warned me to be careful. "Why don't we email for a little while and go from there?"

He immediately reached into his jacket and pulled out a small notebook and pen. After quickly writing his address, he tore out the page, handed it to me, and then offered the notebook for me to write my address for him. Then he glanced at his watch and reluctantly said, "I must go, Christina, but I want you to know that I like you, and I want to see you again as soon as you say, okay?"

He walked me back to my car, said goodbye, and headed off toward the airport. I just sat there for a few minutes to catch my breath.

All the way back to the shop and all the rest of the day, I was so excited I could hardly think of anything else. At the same time, I was confused. *How could I be feeling this way so soon?* As I set up the statue honoring Ray and arranged the new accessories, my mind kept drifting back to the tall southern gentleman stranger. I kept glancing at my laptop, willing it to announce, "You've got mail." Finally, it did, and it was him.

> Hi, pretty lady. It's me, the guy you met at the airport.
> Just wanted to say how much I enjoyed meeting you.
> Brad

I immediately replied,

> Brad, I'm glad to have met you also. It's nice hearing from you.
>
> Sincerely, Christina

Chapter 4

FEBRUARY TO MARCH, YEAR ONE
WILLIAMSBURG, VIRGINIA

Over the next week, Brad and I exchanged numerous emails. As we corresponded daily, his short notes became the highlight of my days. I enjoyed hearing his stories of flying across the states to check on various projects, and I liked telling him about my days in the shop. It reminded me of the way Ray and I used to talk. I reluctantly admitted I was as intrigued with Brad as he seemed to be with me, and I was delighted when he asked for my phone number. Sure enough, that morning, not long after I had written him back, my cell phone rang. *Oh, it's Brad! Darn, of all days to have a store full of people with Ellen running late and Janet out sick.* I let the call go to voice mail and turned my smile back to my customers, but my mind was urging them to buy and leave.

When the store door opened yet again, I saw that Ellen had finally arrived.

"Oh, Ellen! Please help Mrs. Adams find a picture to go with her new sofa." I knew Ellen was puzzled at the way I almost grabbed her arm to pull her into the store, but I didn't care. I knew I was unprofessional to hand my customer over to her, but I didn't care. For once, I allowed myself to feel a teenager's excitement as I escaped to my office and hit the callback button. As the rings began, I closed my eyes and sank into a chair. *Oh, please answer.*

"Well, hello there, Miss Larsen." His voice was as smooth and southern as I remembered. He got right to the point: "I want to see those dimples again. Will you have dinner with me this Sunday? We'll go to any restaurant you want, unless, of course," he said jokingly, "you want to cook dinner for me."

"Huh, that won't work—I don't even know how to turn on a stove." I was, in fact, an excellent cook, but I didn't want to fall into the same trap I had with my ex-husband and end up doing all the cooking all the time. I figured it was better to plead incompetence and let it sort itself out the way it had with Ray.

Curiously, Brad didn't respond to my answer; he merely suggested I select a restaurant. "Just don't pick one that's going out of business the way the last one was." He laughed. "Can you come get me at the airport about five o'clock?"

I could, and I did.

As I drove up to the airport entrance on Sunday afternoon, I saw Brad waiting for me. He was holding a small bouquet of red roses. A tall, lanky man, he was almost the complete opposite in looks from Ray. In his gray sports coat, white shirt, and black pants, he was as handsome as I remembered. I could see in his smile how pleased he was to see me as his crinkly eyes traveled down over the sky-blue sheath I was wearing. The intoxicating aroma of the roses filled the car as he slid into the seat and leaned over to press his cheek to mine in greeting, and suddenly, all my senses were on high alert that something momentous was happening.

We drove to a quiet seafood restaurant that overlooked the water in Virginia Beach. We enjoyed delicious food and shared a bottle of good red wine. As I sipped the wine and felt its warmth, I thought I had never tasted better wine—it was even better than the wine from Ray's collection. *Maybe*, I thought, *it's because I'm here with this charming man.*

During dinner, with the help of the wine, we became comfortable enough with each other to talk about our divorces. I told Brad, "I was devastated when I discovered that my ex-husband had played around while I worked nights at the furniture store. Then one day I met a guy named Ray, and his gentleness and loyalty healed my heart and gave me the will to go on with my life. Over time, our friendship grew into marriage plans, until he died suddenly, giving me another heartbreak. I still miss him so much." As my eyes filled with tears, Brad reached over and took my hand.

"Christina, I understand how you must miss him. Ray sounds like a damn nice guy and someone I would have enjoyed knowing."

I quickly realized I needed to change the subject before I started crying. "Please tell me about your family, Brad. I want to hear about you."

"Well," Brad responded, "my wife and I had been married for twenty-five years, when out of the blue, she asked for a divorce. I still don't have a clue what brought that on, but since I wasn't happy either, I agreed. I needed to keep our house and property because I had built a landing strip and hangar for my airplanes, so I bought her a fancy house in Charlottesville. Our divorce was final on Valentine's Day."

Oh my, I thought. *He got his divorce decree on Valentine's Day, the same day I reaffirmed my decision never to fall in love again.*

As we lingered over coffee and dessert, I was focused entirely on Brad's stunning brown eyes and deep voice. The moving shadows from the small candle lamp on the table played over his craggy face, giving him a mysterious look. *He could be a pirate or highwayman. I like him,* I said to myself, realizing I was more and more attracted to him and wanted to know him better.

As we left the restaurant, I was surprised how dark it was outside. With rising concern, I recalled that Brad had told me he didn't have runway lights on his landing strip at home, so he always had to be there before dark or else stay put where he was until morning. Warning bells were now going off full blast in my head. *Oh no, was this his plan all along? To trick me into inviting him home with me?* With a sinking heart that I had allowed myself to fall into his trap, I pulled away from his arm and looked up into his face with alarm.

"Ah, Christina." He cupped his hand around my chin and leaned down to give me a soft, fleeting kiss. "You're so beautiful, Christina. This evening has been marvelous for me, and I'd like nothing better than for it to keep going. But I've got an early meeting tomorrow morning, so I need to find a motel so I can get a few hours of sleep."

Relief washed over me. *Oh, he's fantastic.*

I drove him to a motel near the airport and waited in the car until he came out with a room key. He leaned in through the window to give me another soft but brief good-night kiss and walked away, stopping once to look back and wave. I watched him for a moment, my cheeks flushed with the thrill of being with him.

As I drove away and my heartbeat slowed, a prickly coldness descended on me as I realized he hadn't said anything about calling me. *Will I ever see him again? Is he going to be upset about having to take a cab to the airport in the morning? Is this a case of "Good night. I had a lovely time. It was great meeting you"? Why am I concerned about this or even thinking about it? Maybe,* I thought, *it's because I would enjoy having him as a friend. I hope he calls.*

Chapter 5

MARCH, YEAR ONE
WILLIAMSBURG, VIRGINIA

To my surprise, Brad called me from work the next day and asked if I would pick him up at the airport on Saturday and go to lunch with him. Since I had all but convinced myself I would never see him again, I was delighted to say yes. For the rest of the week, I had to force my mind to concentrate on my work, which included the problem of figuring out how to leave the store on Saturday, which was always a busy day.

Finally, it occurred to me that the business was doing well, and I could afford to hire another employee. I asked Ellen and Janet if they knew anyone qualified who was looking for a job. Janet recommended Martha, a friend with excellent references and many years of retail experience, who could start work right away. As my good luck would have it, Martha was taking courses in interior design and could be a big help to me with the design part of my business too. Just like that, I was free to enjoy my lunch with Brad.

Saturday dawned as a beautiful day full of gorgeous sunshine. I was practically giddy as I washed my hair, painted my toenails a blazing pink, and watched the clock, waiting for the moment I could leave for the airport. Brad was again standing at the entrance, leaning on the doorway with his arms crossed on his chest. This time, he was wearing jeans and a leather jacket, a perfect match to my own outfit. He slid into the car and leaned over to kiss my cheek.

"Mm, mm, milady—don't you look smashing." His eyes swept over me, heightening my senses and making me feel more alive. As we drove away, he pointed to a group of parked airplanes. "That white one with the red stripe is mine. Maybe I'll take you for a ride in it one day." He waggled his eyebrows like Groucho Marx and twirled his pretend mustache.

"Hmm, maybe." I grinned back at him. I knew I was smitten with him, but I also didn't really know much about him. For all I knew, he was riding to the airport on a bicycle and just pretending to be a hotshot pilot. Even if he had flown in, it could have been someone else's plane. Maybe his story about owning a business was just talk. *Be smart, Christina.* I tried to keep my wits about the situation and not be unduly suspicious of someone as nice, generous, and smart as Brad seemed to be, especially since I was so attracted to him physically. All the same, it was okay to be skeptical until proven otherwise. *And besides,* I told myself sternly, *you're never going to fall in love again, remember?*

We drove to a cozy café I knew next to a beautiful little park. Since the day was sunny and warm, we ate on the patio, where we could see daffodils blooming beneath budding dogwood trees and hear birds calling to each other.

"Oh, that reminds me," Brad said as he reached into his pocket and pulled out something that he kept cupped between his two hands. Then he held his hands out to me and opened them. "Ta-da!" He revealed a small carved bird exquisitely painted in a folk-art style. "I saw it and thought of you."

I was enchanted with his thoughtfulness and beamed at him as I held the tiny bird to my heart.

After our lunch, we took an ambling walk in the park, holding hands and talking until it was time for me to drop him off back at the airport.

"Listen," he said, "I've got a big project upstate that I'll be working on for the next two weeks, so I'll be tied up during the week, but I sure would like to see you again next Saturday, just like today—can you do that?"

"Of course. My business keeps me busy too, so I understand." The arrangement was a huge relief to me since I was determined to move slowly in the relationship. I liked him more and more each time we met, but I was not going to give myself permission to fall in love, not even if I knew he really was telling the truth about himself.

When I got back to my shop, I set the little bird next to the wooden statue Holly had given me. Every time I looked at them during the next week, they made me smile. I could hardly wait to see Brad again. Thank goodness business was good, so the week went by quickly.

We met for lunch on the next two Saturdays. I would pick Brad up from the airport, and then we'd go to the same cozy café. From week to week, we watched the buds on the dogwood trees open, first to green and then to brilliant white. In the park, the tulips began to bloom, and the azalea buds appeared. As we experienced the unfolding of spring, we told each other snippets of our stories—what our childhoods had been like, our favorite subjects in school, our teenage misadventures, and our first music concerts. I told him about my family. It was small and close-knit, and my father had died in a car accident when I was barely a teenager. My mother still lived in our family home in Wilmington, North Carolina. My sister had married her high school sweetheart, and she lived in Wilmington too. I had loved school, especially art, so I'd gone on to college and majored in interior design.

Brad was from a well-to-do family that lived in the city of Charlottesville. He had been a rebel growing up, preferring the outdoors and avoiding school as much as possible.

"Yes, sir," he said, taking an exaggerated breath in and out. "Give me the air, the sky, and the ocean any day over being cooped up inside." I could believe that—my original impression that he looked like a cowboy had only strengthened in the time I had known him. Then he looked at me sideways and grinned.

"You know, though, it was mostly about getting away from my mother and her nagging." She was, he explained, an artist who was more interested in her work than she was in her children, especially him, since he was such a goofball and hadn't excelled academically the way his two older brothers had. His dad was okay, but he always had been gone somewhere on business and hardly ever home. My heart ached with sorrow for the lonely little boy I imagined he must have been.

So, Brad continued, sneaking a glance at me, he had been a wild child for a long while until a family friend who owned a construction business had convinced him to come work with him after school and summers. At first, the job had been just an excuse to be outside instead of inside doing homework at a desk, but gradually, he'd come to enjoy the mental aspect of it too—figuring out the logistics of how to plan for jobs and then bidding for them. When his friend had retired, it had been only natural that he took over the business, despite being only in his twenties.

Brad also told me of eloping with his high school sweetheart, Nancy, when he was eighteen and of the birth of their daughter, Laura, six months later. His mother had been so upset and angry with him that she had refused to speak to him or meet his wife and baby for more than a year. Laura was now twenty-five years old, married, and a full-time mother to her two-year-old daughter, Dawn. Her husband, Sam, was a musician who didn't make much money, so their financial situation was grim.

"It irritates me that Sam only works a few nights a week playing drums and sleeps most of the day instead of having a job that brings in a steady paycheck. I also have a twenty-one-year-old son named Martin, who works for me. He has great business potential, so I'm grooming him to take over my company someday."

As I listened to Brad talk about his children, my mind wandered to my childless state. When I was married, I had been too busy working to have a baby. I was even busier later, getting my design business established and making it a success. But in the deepest back rooms of my mind, I knew I had secretly anticipated that sometime, somehow, Ray and I would have a family—but that hope had died with Ray.

Brad stopped talking and said, "Christina, you look like you're lost in your thoughts."

"Sorry, Brad," I said. "My mind drifted off for a moment, thinking about something I need to do for work."

"That's it—no more talk about my children. But speaking of your work," he said with a grin, "I'm going to make you an offer you can't refuse. I want to fly you to Atlanta to meet a guy I know who makes beautiful lamps—I bet you could sell a dozen in a week. What do you say?"

"Um, no?" I cringed inside at the thought of being in a little plane with him. He said he was an ace pilot, but how did I know if that were true?

"Oh, come on—wouldn't you like to fly in a private jet?"

"Jet?" My eyes widened. "But I thought you only had that white plane you showed me." I fluttered my eyelashes coquettishly and put my hand to my throat. "And besides, I don't know you well enough to go on a trip like that with you."

"Yes, jet—I have one, and I have a copilot too, my little southern belle, so you'll be properly chaperoned. Ah, come on," he said, turning me toward him and holding both my hands in his. "Where's your sense of adventure? It'll be fun. We'll go down, meet the guy, have a nice lunch, and I'll have you back home before dark. You're not afraid, are you?"

"Um, yes?" We both burst out laughing.

Then, still holding my hands, he got down on one knee and said, "Please, dear Miss Christina, would you do me the very great honor of allowing me to escort you to the great city of Atlanta?"

"Hmm." I could feel my dimples twinkling as I responded in my best southern accent, "How can I resist such a heartfelt plea? Very well, Mr. Brad. I'll go to Atlanta with you."

"You won't regret it, sweetheart. It'll be fun," he said as he rose and tucked my hand onto his arm. "I have a break in my work this coming week, so let's go this Wednesday. I'll have my copilot, Graham, meet you at the airport to wait for me until I get there. He's Martin's friend, so he's young, but he's an excellent pilot—you'll like him."

I was surprised to think about Brad having a copilot. *Maybe he is a hotshot guy. Maybe he does own two airplanes.* I was having a little trouble believing it because he hadn't struck me as someone who had a tremendous amount of money. He seemed more like a regular, slouchy John Wayne kind of guy who hung around airports, but it was gradually dawning on me that I might be wrong.

Chapter 6

MARCH, YEAR ONE
ATLANTA, GEORGIA

Over the next few days, I alternated between elation over what I felt would be a fun day with an exciting man and mounting concern that I shouldn't be flying off into the wild blue yonder with someone I barely knew. My logical mind questioned all of this, and I fought with myself as if I had been split into two people. I looked at the photo of Ray on my bedside table. *Oh, Ray.*

I could hear him as clear as day: "Now, Christina, where's your gumption? The man hasn't given you any reason to think the FBI wants him, has he? You've flown in airplanes before, yes? So what's the problem?"

Nothing, I guess, I thought. *Except that somehow, it seems like a bizarre thing to do.*

Nevertheless, when Wednesday came, I dressed with care in a beige suit, my highest heels, and a flowered scarf draped across my shoulders. I smiled at my reflection, anticipating Brad's appreciation of how I looked.

At the airport, I had barely sat down in the waiting room, when I saw a young man walking toward me with a big smile and a coffee cup in each hand.

"Hi. Are you Christina?" he asked as he handed me a cup. "I'm Graham." As we waited, I asked him about being Brad's copilot. "Oh yes, Brad flies the Baron and the Cherokee himself when he's checking on jobs close to home, but I help fly the Gulfstream when he goes on longer trips."

I was surprised and asked, "He has three planes?"

"That's right, and he's an excellent pilot too," replied Graham. I knew even a small plane was expensive, but I could understand why he would need one as a company vehicle. But a jet? Why did he need a jet? And how could he even afford one?

"Oh, here he comes!" Graham stood and motioned me over to the window. "See him up there in the sky? He's lining up with the runway so he can land." Within a few minutes, Brad had done just that and taxied up to the terminal where we had gone outside to meet him. The plane, which was white and had a sharply pointed nose, was much larger than I had anticipated. I was both surprised and excited to see him smiling and waving at me from the cockpit. Airport attendants ran to the plane, and one of them placed a red carpet at the foot of the exit stairs. I was astonished. I felt like a princess as Graham escorted me to the red carpet and helped me climb the steps into the plane.

Brad welcomed me aboard with a big hug. The plane had a luxurious and spacious interior, with several large white leather passenger seats. After Brad got me seated and comfortable for the trip, he joined Graham in the cockpit, and a few minutes later, we were off and in the air. I was amazed I was the only passenger. *Like a movie star.* I grinned to myself.

A few minutes into our flight, the plane started to bounce around a bit. I had always heard people say how rough flying in a small plane was, so I wasn't concerned and assumed the bumpy flight was normal. I had brought along a paperback book, and I tried to keep my mind on what I was reading instead of the ups and downs of my stomach. Eventually, the flight got smoother.

I had only read a few pages before we arrived in Atlanta. When Brad guided me to the door of the plane, I experienced the exciting red-carpet event again. A rental car was waiting for us, and as we drove to his friend's warehouse, he explained that

Dave was an old school chum and a friendly and talkative guy. It turned out he was also a jokester. When Brad introduced us, Dave looked straight at me and said, "This one"—he elbowed Brad—"I always thought would end up living under a bridge somewhere. Who woulda thunk he'd end up a multimillionaire?"

I looked at Dave sharply. *Is that true?* I wondered.

"Huh," responded Brad. "You've done well yourself, Dave." I agreed as I looked around at his displays. I'd thought the lamps Brad had told me about were going to be from a one-man organization, but it turned out Dave had an extensive network of craftsmen and kept shops all over the country supplied with one-of-a-kind merchandise.

"Oh, these two are beautiful! Exactly what I need for my design business." After I paid for the lamps and Dave packed them up, we said our goodbyes and went to lunch.

Back at the airport, Brad and Graham got the plane ready while I relaxed in my comfortable seat with my eyes closed and thought about the new things I had learned about Brad. I felt his warmth brush by me and opened my eyes as he sat down beside me and took my hand.

"Aren't you supposed to be driving the plane?" I teased.

"Nah, the weather's better now than it was this morning, so Graham can handle it—he's a big boy. Did you have a good time?"

"I did indeed. It was so sweet of you to go to all this trouble for me."

He rubbed the back of my hand with his thumb and raised his eyebrows at me. "Don't you know being with a classy lady like you makes me look good? Ole Dave couldn't believe you'd even have anything to do with me."

"Oh, he was just having some fun with you." I laughed. "You're as smooth as they come."

We spent a little while talking about what we had seen and done that day, until we were almost back to the Williamsburg airport. Brad returned to the cockpit until we landed and then came back to help me off the plane. Once again, I emerged like royalty onto the red carpet, obligingly trailed by Graham with his arms around my two lamp boxes. Brad followed us out to give me a brief goodbye kiss and then leaped back up the stairs and pulled them up. Graham and I quickly walked to the terminal. When I turned around, Brad was already in the cockpit, waving to me. As I watched, he taxied out to the runway and took off.

When the plane became a speck in the sky, I turned to Graham with a bright smile. "Shall we go?"

Chapter 7

MARCH TO MAY, YEAR ONE
RIVERWOOD ESTATE AND
WILLIAMSBURG, VIRGINIA

After the trip to Atlanta, Brad and I continued meeting for lunch on Saturdays through April and into May. He frequently asked if I wanted to do something else besides our usual café and park routine, but I felt our relationship was still casual, and I wanted to keep it that way. I hadn't been with anyone but Ray for a long time, and I wasn't ready to let the world know I was moving on after his death.

I thoroughly enjoyed the time Brad and I spent together getting to know each other. I loved hearing him talk about his life and his work, but I was becoming more and more interested in his touch. Our goodbye kisses were lasting longer and becoming more passionate, and I thought about him all the time. Although I was beginning to feel that our relationship could turn into something serious, I still felt uneasy about not knowing anything about him. I had a friend who was a bank manager, so I confided in her and asked if she could find out any information about Brad. She did a little digging and discovered that his business had a high Dun and Bradstreet business performance rating, and there was nothing negative about him personally. Her advice to me was to go for it. Knowing that made me feel more secure about him. Even so, I still told myself just to enjoy his pursuit and not fall in love.

The next Saturday, when I pulled up in front of the airport, Brad slid into the passenger seat and directed me to park the car in the lot. As soon as I parked, he immediately jumped out, opened my door, and pulled me out.

"C'mon. I left something on the plane, and I want you to walk back with me to get it."

"What is it?"

He waggled his eyebrows and said, "I'll tell you when we get there." He put his arm around my waist and hustled me over the tarmac to the white airplane he had pointed out to me before as being his plane.

"C'mon. I want you to get in with me, but the door only opens on the passenger side, so I have to get in first and pull you in, okay?"

I was unsure what he was doing but nodded in answer. He climbed onto the wing of the Baron's passenger side, got into the plane, and reached down to help me climb to the wing too. After he was in the pilot's seat, he pulled me into the copilot's seat. As soon as I got settled, he reached across me to close and lock the door. Almost simultaneously, he started the engines, checked the gauges, and asked the tower for clearance to take off. I jokingly slapped at him. "Help! He's kidnapping me!"

"You're so right, sweetheart." He grinned at me. "How do you like it so far?"

As the engine revved up, I put my hands over my ears against the roar and crossed my eyes at him in mock protest. I was a little scared, but I remembered how he had flown the jet through inclement weather when we went to Atlanta, so I figured a sunny day should be a piece of cake for him.

After we had been airborne for a few minutes and my nerves had calmed down, I was surprised to find I was enjoying the ride. Brad was having a little fun showing off for me, making the plane dip from side to side so that I would clutch his arm and scream. He followed the path of the James River below us, pointing out various projects he had done. In no time, he made a full turn away from the river over what looked to me to be miles and miles of fields surrounded by woods. I could see several buildings on either side of a dirt lane leading from the river up to a clump of big trees in the center of the fields. As we swooped lower, I leaned forward and saw a huge house in the middle of the trees, with a narrow paved road leading away to a two-lane highway beyond. There was a landing strip.

"Oh my God, Brad!" I screamed and grabbed his arm. "This is your house!"

"It sure is, sweetheart." He grinned. "What do you think?" He made another turn to circle the property again. "There are two hundred thirty-four acres altogether. See the cows over there?" He dipped the wings toward a scattering of brown cows. "A neighbor rents the land for his cows to graze on—keeps the grass mowed," he joked. I saw a small building that Brad said was the guesthouse. Then I noticed a tennis court and swimming pool with a pool house.

"A swimming pool! You have a swimming pool?" I was awestruck.

"I sure do, sweetheart." He cut his eyes across my chest. "I sure hope you have a bikini, because you're going to be spending a lot of time in that pool if I have anything to say about it." He pointed out the window. "See the two houses between the pool and the river? The first one is where Laura lives, and the other one is where Martin lives."

"Your children live with you?"

"Well, not exactly," he answered. "I see Martin at work most days, so when we come home, we go our separate ways."

"Does Martin commute with you in the plane?"

"No, I'm usually going all over to different job sites every day, and Martin oversees the central office, so he drives to work. When Laura worked for me, I saw her every day too. Now that she's staying home with Dawn, they walk over to visit me a few times a week."

As we continued flying over the property between the house

and the main highway, I got a better view of the landing strip and the hangar where he housed his planes. I noticed a small plane and asked if that plane were also his.

"Yes, that's a Cherokee," he answered. "I use it for work mostly."

I thought, *So that's the third plane—the Cherokee.*

"Last week, when Graham and I were waiting for you at the airport, he told me you had three planes. I'm learning that planes have names like cars have names."

"That's right, and I hope you'll soon be the pilot in those planes so I can sit back and relax and enjoy the flight," said Brad. He turned the plane and followed the narrow driveway back up to the house. I could now see that the trees surrounding the house were huge magnolias. They were magnificent, and the beauty of the house and grounds won me over immediately. Bright magenta azaleas were in full bloom and surrounded the house closely as foundation plantings. I could understand now why he wanted to continue living there after his divorce. It was true he needed the airstrip, but the property itself was too beautiful to give up.

"Oh, Brad. It looks like something from *Gone with the Wind!*"

He chuckled. "Well, you know, little lady, I always fancied myself as Rhett Butler." He cocked his eyebrow and pushed out his lower lip in a Clark Gable imitation. "I've always wanted to stand by the front door and say, 'Frankly, my dear, I don't give a damn.'"

Putting my hand on my hip, I responded in my best Scarlett voice, "Well, my dear Brad, just so you know, that kind of sass won't work with this southern girl."

"Now, aren't you the witty one?" he said, and he headed back toward Williamsburg, where we had a late lunch at our favorite café.

As we ate, Brad told me more about acquiring his historic house, named Riverwood, which had been built in 1780. "I felt like one lucky guy when I bought it when I was only thirty-three years old. Unfortunately, the house is disqualified from being on the National Register of Historic Places because the previous owner updated the kitchen and bathrooms."

"Wow, Brad, you have a treasure there," I said. After seeing and hearing about his impressive estate, I mentioned that although I rented the townhouse I lived in, I owned a house that I rented to a professional couple. "Sometime when we're out riding around, I'll show it to you. It's in the Kingsmill gated community."

After we finished our lunch, Brad reminded me we needed to head back to the airport so he could get home before dark. By the time we arrived at the airport, the daylight was almost gone. He told me goodbye and sealed it with a long, passionate kiss that sent electrical thrills throughout my body. As his plane faded in the distant sky, I wished he could have stayed with me longer.

Chapter 8

Brad called me the next day after our impromptu visit to Riverwood. "Listen, sweetheart," he said. "Once a week just isn't going to be enough for me anymore. I like you, and I want to spend more time with you. What do you think about that?"

My rational inner voice tried to check in with me, telling me to slow down, but I squashed it like a bug. I was thrilled. "That's great. I'm looking forward to spending more time with you too."

"I'm happy to hear you feel that way, sweetheart, because I've thought about this all night, and here's what I want to do. I'm going to be working near Smithfield for a while, so instead of going back home every night, I'm going to stay a few nights every week at the Smithfield Station. And instead of my always coming to you, I want you to come over here some nights after work. How does that sound to you?"

"Wonderful! I'll be able to take the Jamestown ferry to beat the highway traffic." The hotel was just across the river from Williamsburg in the historical district of Smithfield.

"And by the way," he added, "I want you to start this tonight."

I was trembling with excitement as I drove to Smithfield to meet him that evening. As I parked in front of the hotel and saw him smiling at me from the porch, I thought he was the most handsome man I had ever seen. He bounded down the steps, opened the car door, pulled me into his arms, and kissed me hard.

"I thought maybe you had changed your mind," he said when we finally came up for air.

"Oh no. I couldn't wait to see you again."

"C'mon. Let's eat," he said as he tugged me onto the porch. "I'm starved. We'll eat here at the hotel restaurant. I've already reserved a table for us that overlooks the Pagan River—you'll love it."

I did. We started our evening off with a scrumptious appetizer and a bottle of fine red wine, but Brad had me so smitten that I hardly knew what I was eating. We were so happy to have that extra time to be together that we couldn't stop talking. Since we were both so zealous about the challenges of running a business, we had to be careful not to let that topic dominate our conversation. I loved the excitement in Brad's voice as he spoke of how much he loved flying and his plan for me to get my private pilot's license. We admired the beautiful water view and talked about how much we both loved boating and other outdoor activities. We were all smiles and held hands during the entire meal.

After dinner, we walked down the street past beautiful old homes to the quaint downtown area and browsed through a few shops. When I admired a pair of antique opal earrings, he promptly bought them for me. My heart swelled with joy.

Holding hands, we strolled back to a small marina next to the hotel and out onto a dock where boats were moored. Brad stopped in front of a big sailboat named *Gone with the Wind.*

"Didn't you say my house reminded you of this movie?"

"What do you mean?" I asked. "Is this your boat?"

"Nah, it's just somebody's boat. The owner won't care if we borrow it for a while."

Shocked, I tried to pull back. "Brad! What are you doing? We can't go on a stranger's boat like that."

"Of course we can," Brad responded. "Don't worry about it. People do things like this all the time." He stepped off the dock into the boat and then turned to put his hands around my waist. He lifted me onto the boat and led me to a seat at the back where we could look out over the river. He put his arm around me, drew me tightly to his side, and then threw his other arm out in an expansive gesture and took a deep breath. "Look at that view! Smell that air! Isn't this great?"

Although I was nervous and fully expected we would be arrested for trespassing, I had to admit the view was beautiful, and the gently rocking boat was hypnotic. When a policeman didn't materialize, I finally took a deep breath and let myself lean against him and enjoy the sound of the water lapping against the boat and the smell of the salty air. We watched the clouds turn pink and lavender as the sun set. Reluctantly, we walked back to my car and said sweet goodbyes. Brad had an early meeting, and I still had my daily paperwork to do.

"Listen," he said as he helped me into the driver's seat. "I'm going to rent a car on Saturday and drive over to see you. I'm going to take you to a nice restaurant, so dress up sexy for me, and wear some high heels." He then made me promise on scout's honor to come back the next day, which I did—and the next day too.

We settled into the routine of having dinner at the hotel, walking past the old houses, and then sitting on "our" boat until the sun began to set. I was still apprehensive about trespassing, but it seemed Brad was right about no one caring, so I gradually relaxed and just enjoyed it.

On Saturday, Janet, Ellen, and I were getting the store ready to close. I was trying hard not to look at the clock for the millionth time, when I glanced up and saw Brad walk through the front door. My heart immediately started pounding in my ears, and I rushed out from behind the counter to greet him. Brad slowly spun me around and gave a whistle in appreciation of my hot-pink sundress and strappy heels. Janet and Ellen broke out in spontaneous laughter.

"C'mon, ladies," he said, tapping his watch. "Time's a-wastin'."

With that, they rushed out with big smiles and thumbs-up for me as I closed and locked the door behind them.

"You are so beautiful," he said as he slipped his arm around my waist and gently pushed my hair back behind my ear on one side. "Ah, you're wearing the opals." He bent and kissed my neck just below the earrings. Then he surprised me by giving me a little slap on my rear and said, "C'mon, woman—let's go eat."

Brad had leased a town car, and he took me to an upscale restaurant I had been to many times with Ray. As luck would have it, several couples who had been friends with Ray were there. When they saw me walk in on Brad's arm, they immediately waved and came over to hug me. When I introduced them to Brad, I was pleased to see approval in their eyes. With that assurance, I felt confident enough after dinner to invite him back to the townhouse I had moved into after Ray died. It was a small but comfortable residence in a quiet neighborhood near my business. After I'd graduated from Parsons, I'd started collecting good antique furniture. Ray had helped me by giving good investment advice, so I'd been able to acquire a few more pieces, plus wonderful works of art. Over the last year, I had gradually pulled it all together, so now I had a warm, colorful nest. I had not invited any other man into my new home before, so I was a little hesitant as Brad took the key and opened the door for me. I turned to watch his face as he stepped in behind me and looked around.

"Ah, Christina," he said, nodding. "This is nice. Very nice."

"Why, thank you, Mr. Brad," I said. "Now, come on to the kitchen, and let's get some coffee before you have to go back to the hotel." I was aware of his surprise at my words, but he smiled, caught my hand, and drew me to his chest. He put his hands on my shoulders and looked deeply into my eyes.

"Sweetheart, you are the most exquisite creature I've ever met. What would it take to make you mine?"

I was speechless as he slipped one arm around my waist and pulled me tightly against him. He kissed my lips softly and then nuzzled my neck. For one glorious minute, I gave myself up to mindlessness, and then I stepped back deliberately and tugged him into the kitchen.

"C'mon," I said brightly. "Let's make that coffee." I grinned at his expression. He seemed shocked that I had resisted him.

The next morning, I was in the back studio, working, when my employees walked in with huge grins on their faces.

"Look what just came for you!" Ellen exclaimed, holding out a long florist's box. "Open it! Who's it from?"

Oh, Brad, I thought. *You've surprised me again.* I had received flowers before but never at my workplace. Ellen and Janet pretended to swoon when I took the gorgeous long-stemmed red roses out of the box.

"Oh, you silly girls." I laughed. "Go find something to put these in." When the flowers were safely in a vase, I put them on the counter with the bird and the little wine man statue.

The next morning, I was surprised to receive another dozen red roses—and again the next morning and the next. I received flowers every workday for several weeks. That kind of thing only happened in the movies, so it generated considerable interest from my customers. As the roses filled my store, taking up every available space, every time I talked to Brad, I playfully asked him to stop sending them or at least to have them delivered in vases. After that, the roses arrived in vases, and I eventually acquired so many vases that I returned them to the florist. When I arrived at the florist loaded down with boxes of vases, the receptionist excitedly called all the floral employees up to the front desk to meet the lady who was getting the roses every day.

The presence of the beautiful flowers and their intoxicating aroma did what Brad intended, because I found myself constantly smiling and thinking about him. In fact, I had to admit he was the only thing I thought about those days.

Chapter 9

Brad began to pursue me in earnest. My excitement level was building, and I couldn't stop thinking about him. Gone were the days of early Saturday lunches at the café and walks in the park. I visited him at the Smithfield Station for two or three weekday evenings, and he visited me on Saturdays and Sundays. He now told me how he wanted me dressed when we were together, and I was pleased to comply—it thrilled me to see his pleasure in looking at me when I did. After our Saturday night dinners, we went back to my townhouse, which led to more intimacy. Even so, I somehow managed to resist his most ardent overtures with a light touch so that he would often burst out laughing at my antics.

One Saturday evening, Brad and I were cuddled up on the sofa, watching a TV movie, when the program was interrupted by a weather alert for severe thunderstorms with heavy rain, high winds, and lightning strikes. Brad looked at me sheepishly and asked, "Is it okay if I spend the night here on the sofa instead of driving back to the hotel in this bad storm?"

"Of course you can stay here," I said. "I would be worried sick about you if you left in this terrible weather."

After the movie ended, we decided it was bedtime, and I carefully made up Brad's bed on the sofa. I kissed him good night and told him, "I hope you sleep well."

I slept with one eye open that night, fully expecting him to come creeping into my bedroom, but he stayed on the sofa, just as he'd said he would. He was gone the next morning when I got up, but he had left me a nice note thanking me for my hospitality. *What a real gentleman*, I thought.

The next time I saw Brad, I reminded him he had told me his birthday was July 15. "That's this coming Saturday. I'll make reservations for a birthday dinner, and it'll be my treat."

When Brad arrived at my townhouse on Saturday, I had a store-bought birthday cake waiting for him.

"What a surprise!" he exclaimed happily. "I haven't had a birthday cake in forever. Did you bake this cake for me?"

"Of course," I said, even though the cake was in a grocery store box. "Don't you remember I told you I didn't know how to cook?"

He began arriving earlier and earlier on the Saturdays when I had scheduled appointments, hanging around the store, teasing and joking with my employees and me, and just generally interfering with my concentration and professional decorum. I finally gave up and arranged for Martha to work on Saturdays so she could handle all design appointments and finish the day with Ellen and Janet.

"Are you happy now, Mr. Brad? From now on, I can be off almost every Saturday."

He immediately scooped me up into his arms and swung me round and round. "You won't regret this. I promise."

It pleased Brad greatly that he had been able to wean me from my work, and over the next several Saturdays, he took me to the beach, on bike rides, and to movies to prove to me that I had made the right decision. One rainy Saturday, he took me to three movies in a row. Then he began to wear down my determination to work even an occasional half day on Saturday to catch up on paperwork by showing up at the store before noon and urging me to leave. "If only, my love, you didn't ever have to work at all on Saturdays."

After a few hectic weeks of play-fighting him about it, I finally threw up my hands in mock despair and said, "I give up! You win! I'll let the girls take care of the shop all day on Saturdays, and I'll do the paperwork another time."

As a surprise to me for giving up working on Saturdays, Brad flew us to Wilmington the next Saturday so he could meet my mother, Elizabeth. When we arrived at her house, Mother said, "I'm so glad to meet you, Brad. Every time I've heard from Christina lately, all she talked about was the nice guy she met at the airport."

"It's nice meeting you too," Brad replied. "It was my lucky day when I met your beautiful daughter. We're only a short flight from here, so you'll be seeing us often."

After that, on most weekdays, Brad started coming straight to my townhouse from the airport to shower and wait for me to get home. He also picked up takeout from a seafood restaurant for our dinner. One evening, he confessed to me that when my phone rang before I got home, he answered and told any male callers he was my houseboy. Since I had met Brad, I had continued to receive calls from men I knew. Sometimes salesmen who visited my shop had called to see if I would have dinner with them while they were in town, but the calls had recently stopped, and I had wondered why—now I knew.

It was getting harder and harder for him to leave and make the drive back to Smithfield late at night. One evening, he said impulsively, "I want to spend the night with you and not sleep on the sofa this time."

It only took a moment's thought for me to decide I was ready for our relationship to move forward to the next level. I had no reason not to let Brad sleep over and share my bed. I gave him a smile, took his hand, and led the way to my bedroom. Before we took a long, hot shower together, he slowly undressed me, calling me his package he wanted to unwrap.

"Where's your lotion? You look like you could use a massage. I've been told I'm quite an expert."

Our first night of sleeping together was wonderful. I was

impressed with Brad's gentleness and his concern for my pleasure. Sex with him felt natural and connected. The way he caressed me after our lovemaking made me feel loved and cherished. Falling asleep in his arms was all I had dreamed of recently.

Our relationship had become a priority for both of us, and we spent more and more time together. When my friend Kelly invited me and a guest to her mid-August formal wedding, I naturally asked Brad to go with me. He didn't hesitate before responding, "It would be my honor to go with you."

When the wedding day arrived, Brad came to my townhouse dressed in a tuxedo. I almost fainted when I saw how handsome he looked. After giving me a hello kiss, he told me how exceptionally beautiful I looked in my new strapless light raspberry formal gown. I had French-braided my hair and was wearing the opal earrings he had given me.

We arrived at the church on time, and I was proud to introduce Brad to my friends attending the wedding and reception. Many guests told us what a spectacular couple we made. When the time came for Kelly to throw her bridal bouquet, she threw it directly to me. Likewise, Kelly's new husband, Jim, threw the garter directly to Brad. The clapping and cheers from the other guests made me feel a little embarrassed. I hadn't been trying to catch the bouquet—after all, I was never getting married again.

On the drive home, Brad told me, "You're the happiest woman I ever met."

It was true. I was deliriously happy as I felt myself falling more and more in love with him every time I saw him. I thought, *My defenses just aren't strong enough to resist this charming man.*

Brad continued to send flowers to the store every Monday and call me every morning before work. My day seemed to go more smoothly after I heard his voice, and I eagerly awaited his call. I also gradually realized he seemed a little unsure of me. When the phone rang for a long time before I answered, he wanted to know why I hadn't picked up right away. I didn't answer the phone at all one time because I was in the shower. To my surprise, Brad seemed upset and drilled me as to why I hadn't answered. I was taken aback by his questions and blurted out that I took morning showers. *Oh my gosh*, I thought. *This is a side of him I haven't seen before.* I realized then that Brad was a tough guy who ran a huge business with an iron fist and expected everyone to do exactly as he said. I didn't want to be on the receiving end of that hard voice again, so from then on, I made sure my cell phone was within arm's reach when I was in the shower.

Chapter 10

SEPTEMBER TO OCTOBER, YEAR ONE
SMITHFIELD AND WILLIAMSBURG, VIRGINIA

The time since Brad and I had met had flown by, and our relationship was now public knowledge. Ray had been gone long enough that I no longer felt awkward about being seen with Brad. Most of our dating was still done in Williamsburg because of my work schedule, but I had traveled to a few work sites with Brad near his home in Lynchburg and to his main office in Charlottesville, where we ate at some of his favorite restaurants.

We were also getting comfortable enough to have lunches at Riverwood. One afternoon when I was there, Brad's son stopped by to give him a business report.

"Martin," said Brad, "I want you to meet someone very special to me. This is Christina Larsen from Williamsburg. And, Christina, please meet my son, Martin."

"It's great meeting you, Christina," said Martin. "I hope to see you again soon—maybe at the Peanut Festival? Dad said he was taking you." Martin then said goodbye and walked quickly out the door, heading for his home after a day's work.

After he left, Brad couldn't say enough nice things about Martin. He told me what a good worker he was and how fast he was learning to run the business, even though he was young. "He quit high school just like me," Brad said. "He hated being cooped up in school all day and decided he would be happier working for me."

On another Saturday afternoon visit at Riverwood, I had the pleasure of meeting Brad's daughter and granddaughter. Brad seemed delighted as he said, "Christina, this is my daughter, Laura, and her daughter, Dawn. Laura, Christina is my very special friend from Williamsburg. She owns an interior design shop that carries a lot of unusual items. I'll fly you down there to shop sometime."

"That would be fun," said Laura. "It was nice meeting you, Christina. I'm sorry to have to leave so soon, but I have to drive Dawn to her friend's house for a birthday party."

After they left, I told Brad, "You have a beautiful family," but seeing Dawn stirred up a tinge of sadness that I had no children of my own.

Brad continued to show me off to the world as his girlfriend every chance he had, introducing me as the Princess. I kept insisting he slow down, telling him, "I'm not in a hurry for anything more." I realized more and more that he was a take-charge person who thought he knew what was best in any situation and for everyone involved.

When Brad invited me to go with him to the Suffolk Peanut Festival, he told me to be at the airport by three o'clock on Friday afternoon. I arrived at the airport on time and waited for him to fly in. When he arrived, I thanked him for inviting me. "This is going to be a lot of fun," I said. "I've seen the festival advertised for years, but my work kept me from going." Brad always had a gift waiting for me when I flew with him, and that day was no exception. I slowly opened the beautifully wrapped gift box and found a gold rope necklace inside. "Oh, Brad," I said. "You're spoiling me."

"You don't know the half of it," he replied. "I'm only just beginning to spoil you, my princess."

Shortly after we arrived at the festival, Brad spotted Martin and his friend Graham. After a brief hello, the guys went off on their own. I had another time-of-my-life experience, drinking cold beer and dancing most of the late afternoon and early evening away on that hot September afternoon. The band was the Beach Boys, who were terrific, as usual. Brad and I both loved beach music and knew most of the songs, so we did a lot of shag dancing.

After the festival, we went to a nice restaurant located in an old house on Main Street in downtown Suffolk. The restaurant was closed when we arrived shortly after nine o'clock, but Brad knocked on the door and convinced the proprietor to let us in. I was waiting in the car, so I didn't hear how Brad persuaded him to open the restaurant for us, but he soon turned around and waved for me to come on.

"How did you accomplish this?" I asked.

"I told them I had a hungry princess in my car who needed a nice honeymoon dinner," he said.

"Bradford Hightower, I wouldn't put that past you for one minute," I said.

We had the whole restaurant to ourselves, and the service was exceptional. By the time we finished eating, it was late, so we decided to stay in a motel in Suffolk for the night. After we made incredible love, I ended the day by falling asleep in Brad's arms but not before I said, "Thank you for making another day in my life so much fun. I'll always remember this."

"You're very welcome, my precious one. Sweet dreams," Brad whispered in my ear.

In October, we continued meeting for dinners at the Smithfield Station, and I spent many nights there with Brad. He came to my townhouse when his schedule would allow, still picking up dinner on the way for us and not leaving until morning. One evening, I said, "My love, do you realize we're practically living together?"

"I hadn't thought of it that way," he responded. "But I'm the happiest I can ever remember being."

My wonderful employees made it possible for me to take longer trips with Brad. They were all so accomplished at running the business when I was away that there were times when I felt I wasn't needed at all. During our travels, Brad insisted on taking me shopping for new outfits and matching shoes. He always teased me about having such small feet.

"Brad, you're just trying to irritate me. Stop it! My feet take me where I want to go," I would retort. He told me over and over that he had never known a woman like me who could put on anything and look good in it.

"The longer I know you, the more amazing you become," he told me.

One afternoon, soon after Brad left my store, he called and told me to go to Alan Furs, a shop a few blocks down the street. "I won't take no for an answer," he said.

After telling Ellen to mind the shop, I quickly headed to the fur store, thinking the whole way there, *What is this guy up to now?* When I arrived, Brad had already left the store, but the manager told me Mr. Hightower had picked out several mink coats for me to try on, and whichever one I chose was already paid for. I tried on all the coats and made my selection. I returned to work wearing my new full-length mink coat, feeling glamorous and enjoying being envied by my employees and customers.

That evening, when I arrived in Smithfield, Brad's eyes bulged when he saw how happy I looked wearing my new coat.

"Mr. Hightower, I can't believe you did this," I said. "It's beautiful but far too expensive!"

"My darling, you're worth every penny that coat cost for making me so happy. I hope you know how much I love you."

"I do! Thank you, my prince, for making me feel like a princess."

Chapter 11

Over time, Brad voiced his concern about my shop being in a strip mall and my being there alone doing paperwork late at night. Then the unthinkable happened.

One warm afternoon in late October, I propped open my shop door to let in fresh air. I didn't have any customers at the moment, so I walked over to look outside and noticed a scraggly-looking young man squatting just to the left of my door. I quickly stepped back inside and quietly pulled the door closed. I told Janet about the guy outside and how uneasy he made me feel, but I convinced myself he could be waiting for someone. There had been no previous trouble in the shopping center, so I didn't panic.

A few minutes later, when I looked again, he had moved to the left several more feet to the corner of the Medicine Shoppe, which was next door to my shop. The next time I peeked out, he was sitting on a hay bale in front of the hardware store on the other side of the Medicine Shoppe. When I checked again, he was gone—I saw no sign of him anywhere. I told Janet, "I'm curious about where that guy has disappeared to, so I'm going to walk to the hardware store to see if someone there saw him and knows what happened to him."

As I entered the hardware store, I met the manager, Jack, who told me the alarm system between his store and the drugstore had just gone off, and he was leaving to see if anything were wrong. I followed him. When we entered the drugstore, I was shocked to see the scraggly man behind the pharmacy counter, holding a knife to the pharmacist's neck. Jack and I quickly backed out and ran to our stores to call the police. A few seconds later, I saw the guy run past my front door. *Thank God I locked it!*

When the police arrived, they couldn't find the robber. The pharmacist wasn't hurt, but he had given the man the drugs and money he had demanded. While we were all standing around on the sidewalk, I was stunned when the insurance agent whose office was on the other side of my shop told me that before I'd moved in, he had been robbed, beaten, and locked in the back room.

That evening, when Brad arrived, I was still shaking as I told him all that had happened. "You're going to get killed!" he exclaimed. "If that guy had had a gun, he could have shot you." Seeing Brad's anxiety, I decided not to tell him about what had happened to the insurance agent.

Brad was already not happy about the apartment complex a block from my townhouse. When he spent the night with me, we usually lay awake talking until the wee hours of the morning, so we could hear all the bangs and bumps of people in the complex coming and going all night. We were often awakened in the morning by tenants trying to start old cars that needed cranking over and over. He called it the ghetto. I understood why he felt that way. Since his vast estate had few neighbors in sight, he wasn't accustomed to living so close to a variety of people.

"Why are you here renting a townhouse when you have a house you could be living in?" he asked.

"Because," I answered, "the rent I get for my house is more than I pay for my townhouse. I have fewer things to take care of here, so my living expenses are lower, and I can put as much money as possible back into my business." Brad never gave up trying to persuade me to move. My response to his persistence was always "I'm comfortable here, it's right across the street from my shop, and I like the way I have it decorated."

After the robbery next door, I was more uneasy about staying late alone in my store. I always helped work the afternoon shift because I needed to be there after closing time to do the endless paperwork. It was vital to keep track of the store's inventory and order new stock as well as keep up with payroll, taxes, and other bills involved with maintaining a corporation in good standing. Doing all of that myself was time-consuming and draining, but I never had been comfortable with other people handling the store's money. I always remembered the advice Ray had given me: I should be the only one who managed the money.

However, after thinking things over for a few days after the robbery, I told Brad, "You know, you're right. I really should move back to my house."

He gleefully gathered me into his arms and said, "I just want you to stay safe, my princess." I was a little disconcerted about the "I won" gleam I thought I saw in his eyes, but nevertheless, I notified the renters that I wanted to take possession of my house.

When Brad remembered that I had a birthday coming up in a few days, he said, "Christina, I want to do something you'll like for your birthday. Have you ever had dinner at the Williamsburg Inn?"

"No, I haven't," I answered. "The only time I've been to the inn was when we walked around the grounds and watched people bowling on the green."

"It's settled then," said Brad with a satisfied smile. "I'm making dinner reservations in the Regency Room at the Williamsburg Inn for your birthday gift."

On the night of my birthday, I dressed in a sleeveless peach-colored dress with a gathered bodice that came up high around my neck and buttoned down the back. It was fitted at the waist and had a flowing full skirt with a slit high up my thigh. With the straps of my gold designer shoes buckled around my ankles, I was ready for my birthday evening.

I had a hard time deciding what to order because everything looked appetizing. While sipping a glass of Chardonnay from the

Williamsburg Winery, I finally selected the inn's signature dish: crab Randolph. Brad ordered chateaubriand, another signature dish. For dessert, we shared hazelnut ice cream cake with marinated strawberries and Kahlua fudge sauce. As we finished the last of our wine, I relaxed back in my chair and smiled warmly at Brad, savoring the moment and thinking how lucky I was to have him in my life.

On the way back home, I thanked him for making my birthday one to remember. "Brad, you have a talent for coming up with exciting things to do."

Chapter 12

By November, I was settled back into my house thanks to Brad's helping me move. I had learned he was a person who made things happen. If he got an idea, he went full steam ahead to fulfill it without any delays. If a decision turned out to be wrong, with his monetary means, he could easily correct his mistake.

As Thanksgiving approached, our life together was beautiful and full of fun and travel to many places I had never been. I occasionally went with Brad to equipment auctions where he could take advantage of businesses that had fallen on hard times and acquire expensive equipment for pennies on the dollar. I was not excited about going, but I did it anyway because I loved Brad, and he wanted me to go with him. The auctions were held outside year-round in open dirt fields with no bathroom facilities. On one trip, I needed to go to the bathroom and asked Brad to take me back to the motel. When he returned to the auction, the item he intended to buy had been sold. I could tell by his demeanor when he returned to the motel that he was not happy with me.

"What's wrong?" I asked. When he said I had caused him to lose out on buying the item he had wanted, I said, "I'm sorry," and I gave him a big hug, which seemed to calm him down. After that, when I went with him to auctions, I waited at the motel.

We had visited my mother many times since the first time Brad flew me to see her. They liked each other, so when she invited us to spend Thanksgiving with her, he was in total agreement for us to go. While Mother was getting the turkey ready to put into the oven, I discovered we were almost out of ice. Brad was restless and said he would like to take a ride around town to see what was going on, so we volunteered to go get a bag of ice. I knew too that being around the good smells of many of his favorite foods was making him hungry.

We decided to stop by the downtown waterfront to enjoy the view for a few minutes and sat down on a bench next to another couple. Brad immediately struck up a conversation with them and learned they were planning a trip to Eleuthera in the Bahamas in January. They invited us to join them there for a few days. Brad excitedly took their contact information so he could finalize trip plans with them later. I was astonished. *How did Brad manage this? He just met this couple, and now we're planning to meet them in the Bahamas for a vacation?* I thought to myself, *This won't happen—the whole thing is just too bizarre.*

The rest of Thanksgiving Day was spent overeating, relaxing, and visiting with my sister, her husband, and my mother. Before we knew it, it was time to leave for home. Tomorrow would be a workday for us.

Chapter 13

DECEMBER, YEAR ONE
RIVERWOOD ESTATE AND
WILLIAMSBURG, VIRGINIA

Shortly after Thanksgiving, Brad and I went to dinner at a lovely restaurant in Virginia Beach. I jokingly made a comment to him that after coming out of a longtime marriage, he would likely want to play the dating game forever. Brad quickly responded that he had loved married life. Not long after that dinner, he called me at work and told me to pick a date or forget it. I wasn't sure exactly where this was leading, but I went along with it and said, "June 9."

That evening, Brad surprised me by telling me to invite my friend Faye to meet us for dinner. I had told him Faye and I often had dinners together when he was out of town, but he had never met her. After Brad poured our wine, he stood up and told her, "I have a big announcement to make. Christina and I are getting married in June."

His statement took me by complete surprise, and I thought, *Oh my God! This guy is serious about us getting married. When he called me today, he was proposing marriage? So that's what picking a date was all about. He was asking me in a very unusual way to choose a wedding date.* I was happy but shocked and incredulous at his announcement.

Faye gave us big hugs and said, "I'm so happy for you. Have you started making wedding plans?"

"Not yet," I said.

"Let me know if I can help," she said.

"Thank you. I'll be in touch," I said.

When Brad excused himself to get another bottle of wine, Faye said, "Wow, Christina. How did you find this gorgeous creature?"

"I don't know! He just fell out of the sky one day."

"I hope you know how lucky you are. Guys like Brad don't come along every day."

"I do know how lucky I am. There's no doubt about it—he's amazing. I never expected to meet someone and be planning my wedding so quickly. My vow to never fall in love and get married again seems to have fallen by the wayside."

Brad returned to the table with a new bottle and asked, "Would you ladies like more wine?" We did and happily continued celebrating our fantastic news for several hours.

A few days after our dinner with Faye, Brad invited his father, William, to meet us at a restaurant for lunch. After we were seated, Brad said, "Dad, I asked you here today to introduce you to Christina and to tell you that she has made me the happiest man alive by accepting my marriage proposal."

His dad was happy for us and said, "Son, it looks like you have done well for yourself. She's so beautiful—and smart too. I wish you both well. Now, how are things going with your work?"

When our lunch was over, his father thanked us for inviting him and said he hoped to see us both again soon. "Stop by the house anytime."

I told Brad, "I think your dad is an okay guy just like you. I enjoyed meeting him. I can see where you got your good looks."

Several days later, Brad called me and said, "I've made an appointment with my personal banker for two o'clock this afternoon. I'll pick you up in time for us to have lunch first. It's crucial that you go to the bank with me, so I won't take no for an answer."

I thought, *What on earth does Brad have up his sleeve this time? Is this going to be another one of his surprises?*

When we arrived at the bank, Mr. Sachs, the banker, already had the paperwork ready for a joint bank account to be opened in our names. All we had to do was sign the papers, and Brad would make a deposit.

"Now, sweetheart, you have no excuse for not selling your business. Any money you need will be available for you in this account. We can live in your house while we're planning the wedding and before we make Riverwood our permanent residence."

My goodness, I thought. *Brad has everything figured out. I just got settled from moving back into my house, and now he's talking about my moving again. I've always been the planner, so this is new to me.*

I began thinking about leaving my business and selling my house. Giving them up was troubling to me, but after much pondering, I became confident in my decision to marry Brad. I was physically and mentally exhausted from working long hours on weekdays and most Saturdays for so many years. I felt in my heart that giving up my independence and becoming a stay-at-home wife was the right thing to do. I yearned to have a family life again. I was further encouraged when Brad told me if I wanted to continue working, I could help him with his business as a salaried employee. Or I could even open another design studio. Then he added, "I don't think you'll have time to work while being my wife."

By December, Brad and I were officially living together in my house. When my employee Martha heard I wanted to sell the business, she immediately asked if she could buy it.

"That would be wonderful, Martha. You're an excellent businesswoman, and I know the business will continue to grow and prosper in your hands. I can't think of anyone else I would rather see take over the helm than you." Janet and Ellen were happy too that Martha would be their new employer. I told Brad how lucky I felt to sell my business without even trying and without having to incur the many expenses involved in hiring a business broker.

Martha and I closed the deal for her to own the business

shortly thereafter. I then had the freedom to start enjoying my new life with Brad. I was thrilled with how my life was turning out. I had found someone to love, even though I hadn't planned to ever fall in love again. I was hopelessly committed to Brad.

Seeing how happy I was, he told me again he had never met a happier person. "How do you stay so happy?"

"You make me happy, Brad."

"Stick with me, Christina. The best is yet to come."

During that period, we started attending a small country Episcopal church near Riverwood. The people we met there were friendly and welcoming, and several couples invited us to their homes for dinner parties and even a Christmas party, which quickly expanded our social life. I soon discovered that one nice thing about living in the country was that people entertained often in their beautiful old homes. Women wore fashionable cocktail dresses, and men wore tuxes or impeccably tailored suits. I noticed too that many ladies in the area wore mink coats to church and sometimes even to the grocery store. *Could this be what inspired Brad to surprise me with a mink coat?*

The two of us spent our first Christmas Day together quietly at my house. I cooked dinner with all the traditional foods: turkey, dressing, pumpkin pie, and other side dishes. Brad gave me a heart-shaped diamond necklace, and I gave him a cashmere sweater. He had wanted to give me a diamond engagement ring, but I asked him to wait until Valentine's Day, which would be just two days before the one year anniversary of our meeting.

After Christmas, I still had things to do to make my house our temporary home, as well as personal and business taxes to take care of. As I did those tasks, I thought to myself the whole time, *It'll be so great to get out from under all this paperwork.*

Chapter 14

Right after Christmas, Brad called Brenda and Joseph, the couple we had met in Wilmington at Thanksgiving, and made plans to meet them in Eleuthera. They were flying commercial, and we were flying in Brad's Gulfstream jet, so we wanted to make sure we would arrive at about the same time.

Brad flew us from Riverwood to Wilmington and then to Palm Beach, Florida. After going through customs and passport control smoothly, we traveled to Eleuthera and met Brenda and Joseph, who had already arrived and were waiting for us at the Governor's Harbour Airport.

They had been to Eleuthera several times before and had recommended we stay with them at their favorite resort. When we entered our room, we were amazed at how beautifully it was decorated in a tropical theme. I opened the door to the balcony and excitedly called to Brad, "Come see this gorgeous view of the ocean!"

We weren't meeting the others for dinner until later, so Brad lay down to take a nap on the king-size bed. He always looked tired after piloting the plane for a long distance. After just a short nap, he would get up rested and looking younger. I realized the enormous burden that Brad carried on his shoulders when we traveled alone without Graham's help. As the sole pilot, he had full responsibility for keeping track of the weather, making sure the plane was fueled and in good maintenance, and ensuring he was well rested and in good health, plus a multitude of other things.

For the next several days, we enjoyed getting to know our new traveling companions as we went sightseeing, ate excellent meals, and just relaxed together. One afternoon, the four of us were sunbathing on the beach. My skin was so fair that I needed a lot of suntan lotion. Brad was delighted when I asked him to apply the lotion on me. Brenda and I preferred to lie on our blanket and talk while the butler kept us supplied with Goombay Smash drinks, but Brad and Joe spent their time swimming. *They don't mind being in the cold water,* I thought. Brad didn't understand how I could be happy just sitting there, so he started insisting I join him in the water.

"I won't take no for an answer!" he shouted. "Come on in, Christina, or I'll come up and get you. The water's warm, so come join me."

I was trying to be a good sport and not make a scene in front of our new friends, so I didn't resist when he ran up, grabbed my hand, and pulled me into the water. As soon as he got me thoroughly wet, he dashed back up to the sand, threw himself down on our blanket, and flashed a devilish grin. I realized he hadn't wanted to play in the water with me—he'd just wanted to prove he could make me get in even though I didn't want to. I wanted to kill him! However, after my body became acclimated to the water temperature, I thought, *I'm in the ocean in January, and it's actually quite nice—so nice I don't want to get out.* I tried to coax Brad to come back into the water with me, but he wouldn't.

Despite my irritation with him, I didn't stay annoyed long—I was otherwise enjoying myself too much. We were staying at a lovely resort, and the views from our room were breathtaking. The food in the dining room was sumptuous, and the service was impeccable.

One romantic night, Brad and I sat on our bedroom balcony

and sipped wine while we looked out over the moonlit ocean. "You know, sweetheart," Brad said, "After we're married, I won't always be able to spend this much time with you. You've been the only thing on my mind for months, and I've got to start focusing on my business again."

"I completely understand," I told him. "I know what it's like to be the boss and run a company. That's something we have in common."

Most evenings, we talked for quite a while before retiring to bed, trying to discover more about each other's needs and commitments. It felt good to me to be building that kind of knowledge along with the romantic side of things.

Brenda and Joseph insisted we take a boating trip with them that would last several days. The captain and tour guide took us along the shoreline of Eleuthera, which was a long, thin island. In some places, we could practically see from one side of the island to the other. We were shocked when we cruised past a couple making love on the beach—in broad daylight! That was a fantasy of mine, but in my dreams, it was always the moon, not the sun, illuminating my naked body.

Our first night aboard the boat was so hot that neither Brad nor I could go to sleep, so we went up to the deck and tried sleeping there in the misty rain. Neither of us got much sleep that night. The next day, the head stopped working, so we had no working bathroom. We all easily decided the best thing to do was to end the excursion and go back to shore and our hotel rooms—the faster the better.

When our vacation time in Eleuthera was over, the four of us drove to the airport together and returned our rental car. Brenda and Joseph waited for their flight while Brad got our plane ready to leave. I had never been to Grand Bahama Island, so I asked Brad if we could go there for one night before we went home, and he agreed. It was late afternoon by the time we arrived and took a cab to the hotel. We stopped in the downstairs bar for a Bahama Mama drink before going to our room to rest before showering and dressing for dinner. The atmosphere in the hotel restaurant was tropical, and we both enjoyed the food they served.

The next morning, Brad wanted to leave early for our trip back home, so I didn't get to see or do as much on Grand Bahama as I had hoped. Because of a severe-weather warning in and around Palm Beach, where we had departed from the United States, we had to divert to the Fort Pierce, St. Lucie, airport. We didn't realize that arriving back in the United States at a different airport would be an issue, but we caused quite an uproar at US customs. They might have thought that since we were a private plane flying in from the Bahamas, we were bringing drugs into the United States. They did not explain why they detained us on the plane while they searched not only the plane itself but also our possessions, even our dirty clothes.

After the customs-delay fiasco, Brad needed to fly straight back to Riverwood to attend a meeting instead of taking me to Williamsburg, so I spent the night there. When his housekeeper, Ida Mae, came to work the next morning, she unpacked our bags and did the laundry from our trip. I knew then that having a lady to cook and clean for me would make being Brad's wife delightful and a lot easier than I had imagined. I already knew what a wonderful cook she was because Brad had occasionally brought her casseroles to my townhouse for our dinners. Our vacation clothes she washed and ironed looked better than when they were brand new. *I could get used to this*, I thought.

I was thanking her as gracefully as I could when Brad got back from his meeting and interrupted me. "Time to head back to Williamsburg. C'mon. Let's go—the plane's waiting."

On the way to the hangar, I told Brad, "Since your housekeeper isn't here on weekends, I'm glad things worked out the way they did so that I got to meet her." When we arrived at my house, I said, "It feels like we're returning home from our honeymoon."

Before I knew it, it was February and then Valentine's Day. That Valentine's Day would be much different from my last one because I would be engaged, and we would be attending a formal charity Valentine's ball. Shortly before Valentine's Day, Brad mentioned that he had purchased my engagement ring but had returned it to the jewelry store and would have to go back to get it. I was busy when he told me, so it didn't really register with me what he was saying, but I thought, *Why did he return it? I must have done something to upset him.* I wasn't sure what would have triggered such a response, so I passed it off that he was just kidding.

During our Valentine's night dinner, he presented me with a four-carat diamond ring in a Tiffany setting. "Oh, Brad!" I exclaimed. "This must be the most beautiful diamond ring in the world! Thank you! I'll wear it with great pride."

Chapter 15

FEBRUARY TO MAY, YEAR TWO
RIVERWOOD ESTATE

The wedding was only a few months away, and I had many things to do. Because it would be the second marriage for both of us, I envisioned a small, intimate wedding. When I mentioned my thoughts to Brad about keeping the wedding small and having a big celebratory party later, he replied, "But, sweetheart, there'll be so many people with hurt feelings if they don't receive a wedding invitation." After much discussion, we finally decided that only a large church wedding would do, followed by a large reception at Riverwood.

I was pleased Brad agreed to have an afternoon wedding rather than a formal wedding after five o'clock because that made planning a lot easier for me. We quickly agreed to ask Reverend Jones to officiate at the Episcopal Church of the Redeemer, the church we had learned to love, where we had made many friends.

Since I was not familiar with Lynchburg, Brad asked his co-pilot, Graham, to drive me to finalize instructions for the caterer, order a wedding cake, and audition bands. My friend Faye went with me to shop for my wedding dress. I tried on many different styles of dresses before she exclaimed, "Oh, you look gorgeous in that one! It looks like it was designed just for you. Brad is going to flip out when he sees you coming down the aisle." With everyone else in the store oohing and aahing too, I knew that had to be the dress I would wear to marry Brad. I had to keep telling myself to calm down and stop acting like a ditzy first-time bride.

Another friend, Amy, went with me to look at wedding invitations. I had an idea of what I wanted, but I wasn't certain. After looking through many books of sample invitations, I saw the perfect invitation for an afternoon wedding. It was old-fashioned looking, with a pastel painting of a horse and carriage in front of a country church that resembled the church where we were going to be married. I told Amy, "This is it. We need look no further." I placed an order for the invitations, and then we headed for a glass of wine and dinner. Most of our conversation was about how well the wedding planning was turning out and where I could find a calligrapher to address the invitation envelopes.

Brad and I took an afternoon off to go shopping for wedding bands. I couldn't find one that complemented my diamond ring, so I decided to use a plain gold band and keep looking for a wedding band I liked. We picked out a plain, wide gold band for Brad, and I had it engraved on the inside all the way around with "I love you. I love you."

The wedding plans continued to proceed smoothly until we started working on our prenuptial contract. Brad and I had agreed long before about the importance of having a prenup. I contacted a local Williamsburg attorney, Shirley Johnson, to represent me. Brad's attorney was Michael Kelton, who handled all his business's legal matters.

The negotiation started between the two attorneys and quickly turned into a nightmare. No matter what terms my attorney asked for, Brad would tell me she was being unreasonable and greedy. The two lawyers were unable to make any headway, and Kelton and Brad made me feel awful about my attorney. They claimed she was being senseless by insisting on what they called absurd terms, though Brad did fulfill one of her requests to take out a $100,000 term life insurance policy on himself with me as the beneficiary.

As the wedding date got closer, the two attorneys stalled in their negotiation. Brad asked me, "Since things aren't working out with your attorney, would you consent to Kelton representing both of us?" I readily agreed.

"It's so stressful negotiating a divorce before we're even married," I told my lawyer. Her parting advice to me was to stash away as much money as I could.

Brad called a day later to tell me Kelton had the prenuptial contract ready for us to sign. "Princess, can you be ready for me to pick you up in about an hour?"

"Yes, Brad," I answered. "I'm looking forward to getting this behind us."

At Kelton's office, I was told to read and sign each page of the contract. The first few pages sounded good to me, but then I came across a paragraph saying, "Item three on the second page is null and void." In other words, that paragraph was a trick that took away all the benefits that had been given to me on previous pages.

I got upset, refused to read or sign anything else, and walked out of the office. On our way home, I pretty much gave Brad hell for thinking I was so stupid. He tried to defuse me by telling me that it wasn't his fault and that it was all Kelton's doing. "He just wants to protect me. Christina, you're one of the most intelligent women I've ever met, as well as the most beautiful." Brad's convincing ways soothed me to the point that when he asked me to go back to Kelton's office, I agreed.

That evening, Brad came home with a strand of pearls and told me, "They're for you to wear on our wedding day."

In the coming weeks, we made several more trips to Kelton's office, and each time, the attorney continued to play the same trick, with the null-and-void line hidden further in the pages. Brad played dumb and kept blaming Kelton. Their plans to deceive me failed because I was not going to sign papers without reading them, so I found the trick every time. By that time, I was so disgusted that I refused to trust Kelton ever again. I was also beginning to think Brad was involved in the scheme too. But when he looked at me with those beautiful, sincere eyes and saw my melting reaction, he knew he was still in control.

"Let's go to our favorite restaurant for drinks and dinner," Brad said when we left the lawyer's office. The restaurant had a piano player, so I requested, as always, that he play "Misty," dedicated to Brad. Everything was lovely that evening between us, and the prenup was not even mentioned.

However, Brad knew he was losing my confidence when I remarked that I had made a mistake in not keeping my own attorney. Since I was an honest professional person who dealt with other honest professionals, I had trusted it would be all right for Kelton to represent both of us when I agreed to Brad's request. Later that week, he asked if I would be willing to talk to another attorney who sometimes helped him with his business matters. I agreed. "I'll do anything to get this unpleasant task settled once and for all."

Unfortunately, nothing got accomplished with the new lawyer either, and the conclusion I came to was that he thought I was a gold digger and that Brad needed protection from me. I felt as if I were living two different lives at the same time, one glamorous and the other out of my control.

The wedding date was coming closer without a prenuptial contract finalized. The problem was taking its toll on all the excitement and happiness of our upcoming wedding. One night, Brad was so angry about it that he threw our wedding gifts onto the driveway, breaking them into a million pieces. At that moment, the shock of seeing him throw our gifts out made me seriously consider calling the marriage off. However, calling it off would have caused much chaos and embarrassment for me, and I was so in love with Brad that I made excuses for him. I thought the reason for his unexpected and surprising bad behavior was probably his anger about having to do so much for his ex-wife when they divorced.

The Monday before the wedding, Brad asked me if I would consent for the two of us to write our own prenuptial contract.

His longtime secretary, Evelyn, could come to Riverwood right then to type it for us as well as notarize the contract. I quickly agreed. "That would be wonderful, Brad. At last, no more involvement with attorneys. We should have done this from the beginning."

That afternoon turned out to be another unpleasant experience. I soon realized Brad and Evelyn were doing the same thing Kelton had tried to do, and I became angry and frustrated yet again. Finally, out of sheer disgust and under duress to end that nightmare, I blurted out for them to put whatever they wanted in the agreement, but the bottom line had to say that after five years, the contract would be null and void, and I would then be entitled to a wife's rights. I wasn't thinking we would ever get a divorce—I didn't even know what a wife's rights were—but I was concerned about what would happen if something unexpected happened to him. My new version of the contract meant I wouldn't receive anything except what he wanted to give me during those first five years. Brad agreed and told me not to worry; he would change his will so that Martin, Laura, and I would each get one-third of the estate—but I never actually saw the will.

After Brad and I signed the prenuptial contract, Evelyn quickly gathered up all the papers, including the original handwritten contract we had signed, and rushed out of the house without giving me a copy. I trusted Brad implicitly and assumed he would give me a copy when things calmed down after the wedding. I was relieved we had finally completed the contract and didn't give it another thought after that.

The wedding excitement continued to build as guests from out of town arrived. My mother, Elizabeth, arrived on Wednesday before the wedding. Aunt Sally and Uncle Calvin drove up from North Carolina on Friday so they could be there for the rehearsal and dinner. That Friday, around noon, Brad flew the Baron to the Lynchburg Airport to pick up my sister, Shirley, and her husband, Jimmy, and bring them to Riverwood.

That evening, our rehearsal dinner was spectacular. Some

of Brad's employees had arranged it for us, and Martin had offered to host it at his house, which had a huge deck. The weather fully cooperated, and everyone had a splendid time visiting, eating, drinking, and talking about our wedding that would be the next day.

Chapter 16

On the morning of the wedding, I was in the foyer, talking with my mother and Faye about last-minute things that needed to be done before we left for the church. As I left them and dashed upstairs, I stepped on something. Looking down at the steps, I saw a small green snake and screamed. A delivery person came running to take the snake away. With a shaky laugh, I told him, "Is this a sign from God? If I weren't in this so deeply, I'd be out of here."

When Brad's employees had asked him what he wanted for a wedding gift, he'd told them a basset hound puppy. An employee brought a cute puppy to the house that morning for us to see. The puppy was nine months old and already well trained by the breeder. Brad and I petted him and couldn't get over how sweet he was. We agreed his name would be Nutmeg because of the coloring of his coat. We finally had to excuse ourselves, so the employee said goodbye and took Nutmeg to Laura's house. She would keep the dog until we got back from our honeymoon.

It was late morning when Brad asked me to go with him to the mall to buy a blouse for me. I couldn't believe my ears and thought, *Where is this weird request coming from?* I told him he would have to go by himself because I was too busy. He left and soon came back with two blouses. *Maybe he's nervous*, I thought. *Maybe this is his way of coping, but it's strange behavior.*

The day continued to bustle with activity. The wedding reception was going to take place at Riverwood, just as Brad and I had planned. The freshly mowed grounds surrounding the house were spacious and beautiful. Everyone was working toward the two o'clock wedding hour. Several muscular men were hoisting tents for the band and dance floor. The food servers were arranging the serving dishes, and the bartender was skillfully setting up bottles at the drink table. The florist truck had already delivered the spring floral arrangements for the garden tables. Sue, the caterer, was setting the tables with white linen tablecloths and napkins. The decorative chair covers matched the flowers in the centerpieces and on the wedding cake she had made. The cake looked like a dream come true. Each of the three tiers contained four layers of yellow cake with strawberries, blackberries, raspberries, and cream between them. The icing was vanilla buttercream with a trail of fresh flower blooms and greenery winding down the three tiers. When I complimented her on the perfect wedding cake, she asked, "What rain plans have you made?"

"None," I said. "Because I have ordered a beautiful day." The previous week had been rainy, but that day had been warm and beautiful so far. All indications were that it would stay that way, so we would have perfect weather for our elegant outdoor wedding reception.

"Good luck," said Sue.

My longtime hairdresser, Robbie, soon arrived from Williamsburg and began working on my bridesmaids' hair before doing mine. He was also staying for the wedding and reception to make sure my hair was always perfect.

I was looking forward to seeing family members I had not seen in a long time and being able to introduce them to Brad. All too soon, the time arrived to leave for the church. On the way there, I was excited but worried that I wouldn't remember the marriage vow I had written. I kept repeating it over and over in my mind: *Brad, you are my best friend and the love of my life. I'm so grateful I get to spend forever with you, because you're a thoughtful, strong, adventurous, kind, and smart man.*

Our wedding party had been instructed to arrive at the church before noon so we could get dressed in our wedding attire there. My ivory wedding dress had a straight satin skirt, and the top was silk covered in lace and sprinkled with sequins. It had a scoop neckline and puffy sleeves, and I was wearing the pearl necklace Brad had given me. My something old was the set of antique pins Robbie had used to secure the spray of flowers in my hair, which he'd styled into a French twist. My something new was the Riverwood house key Brad had made for me, which I had tied on a ribbon inside of my bouquet. The something borrowed was my mother's wedding ring on my right hand, and my something blue was a garter.

Brad's three-year-old granddaughter, Dawn, was the flower girl. She wore a sleeveless A-line tulle and lace dress with a fuchsia waist sash that matched the bridesmaids' dresses. My bridesmaid, Amy, and my maid of honor, Faye, wore fuchsia satin dresses that were off the shoulder. Brad; his best man, Martin; and his two groomsmen all wore dark gray tuxedos.

The thrill of wearing my wedding gown and posing for photographs before the ceremony caused my excitement to keep building. I was happy and thankful that Brad had come into my life and changed my intention to never get married again.

At last, the guests were all seated, and the wedding party had taken their assigned places. As Uncle Calvin and I waited arm in arm in the vestibule of the church, he turned to me with a smile and said, "You aren't going to cry, are you?" My teary eyes and shaky smile gave him my answer. "Ah, I thought so," he responded as he gave my hand a squeeze. When the music changed to "Here Comes the Bride," we began to walk slowly down the aisle. Brad had an ear-to-ear smile on his face as he took my arm, and we turned to face the reverend.

As we had requested, the ceremony was short. We exchanged

our beautiful vows, and Brad gave me a fervent kiss. *We're married!* The congregation stood and clapped for us as we walked quickly down the aisle. We were surrounded by a tremendous feeling of love, happiness, and support.

After posing for more pictures with our wedding party, we were whisked away from the church in a helicopter to Riverwood for our reception. At the house, waiters welcomed us with glasses of champagne while the band played our song, "Misty." Soon our guests began arriving from the church, and we were surrounded by well-wishers. I couldn't resist kidding my friend Paul by saying, "What took you so long to get here? You need an airplane."

The band we'd hired played mostly oldies but goodies. Our first dance as a married couple was to the song "At Last." We had practiced dancing for that occasion when all eyes would be on us, so we were confident we would do okay and look good in our wedding photos. My other requests were "Celebration" and "I Just Called to Say I Love You," my personal favorite. Everyone was dancing and having a good time.

Brad and I stayed busy all afternoon, greeting our guests and thanking them for attending the wedding. All of a sudden, I realized how late it was getting, so I quickly did the bridal bouquet toss and then excused myself to go change into my going-away outfit. I put on a red polka-dot dress with a crinoline slip and instantly became the center of attention when I returned to the reception. Robbie had restyled my hair into an updo adorned with a red flower, telling me, "You look awesome." I felt awesome too. Brad hustled me into the car, and I blew kisses to everyone as we drove away to begin our life as a married couple.

Chapter 17

We drove to the Boar's Head Inn in downtown Charlottesville, where we were to spend our first night as husband and wife. We arrived so late that the hotel restaurant had already closed, so instead of the romantic candlelit dinner I had envisioned, we had to settle for hamburgers at the hotel bar and grill. As we devoured our meal, we recapped the day's events. Finally, I ate my last french fry and leaned back in my chair as Brad reached for my hand.

"I'm exhausted," I said. "Aren't you? I'm so glad we got married early in the day. Just think how late it would be now if we had had an evening wedding. I'm so grateful too that you convinced me to have a big church wedding. We made so many memories today, and my favorite is walking down the aisle to marry you and become Mrs. Bradford Hightower. I love you so much, Brad. I'm the luckiest woman in the world to be your wife."

"Ah, sweetheart," Brad replied, "I'm so happy too to be married to someone as wonderful as you are. You're so beautiful, Mrs. Bradford Hightower."

In the elevator, we kissed all the way to the twelfth floor honeymoon suite.

It seemed we had no more gone to bed than it was time to get up. We needed to be back at Riverwood early that morning to take my sister, Shirley, and her husband to the airport before we left for our honeymoon. I took the time to put on an azure dress from my bridal trousseau that Brad said made my eyes look startlingly blue.

When we arrived back home, Ida Mae had prepared a wonderful breakfast for everybody. After eating, we helped Mother put her things into her car so she could start her trip back to Wilmington. Then we hurried to get Shirley and Jimmy and their luggage into our plane so we could get them to the airport on time.

At last, we were off to start our honeymoon. Brad had planned for us to visit not one but two exciting resorts. Although I had already grown accustomed to the ease a private plane gave us to go different places in a short period of time, I was still impressed by the luxurious freedom it gave us. We first went to the Greenbrier in West Virginia, where we enjoyed a few days of relaxation. I had my first horseback ride and spa visit while Brad played tennis and golf. We then flew to the Cloisters in Georgia for a few days of bike riding and dancing the evenings away. Since I had never been to either of those resorts, I enjoyed all the activity and attention employees and other guests gave us as a newly married couple.

We got home on Sunday afternoon. Brad swung the front door open and insisted on carrying me over the threshold into my new home. When we entered the house, I got the surprise of my life: everywhere I looked, I saw vases of long-stemmed red roses, and on the dining room table were two crystal wine glasses and cold champagne in a silver ice bucket. I was speechless but finally managed to say, "Brad, you know how to make me feel special."

After we were snuggled in bed that night, I said, "I hope I never spend another night without you. Now that I'll be sleeping with you every night, I won't have to sleep in the company T-shirt you gave me. As silly as it sounds, it made me feel safe and close to you." I could tell by the big smile on his face that he was pleased.

I continued. "I'm a little sad that our honeymoon week has come to an end. I had so much fun, but I'm looking forward to starting my new life with you here at Riverwood." *It would be so nice if honeymoons could last forever*, I thought.

"Good night, Christina," Brad whispered in my ear.

Chapter 18

Our new everyday life began the next morning with a crowing rooster as our alarm clock. Since Brad was an early morning person, he got right out of bed, ready to leave the house for work at seven o'clock. I was glad I didn't work anymore and could stay in bed, but all his bumping around while getting dressed and the noise of the departing plane kept me from going back to sleep.

When I got up and went downstairs, I found that Brad had left me a note listing what he thought I should do that day: eat breakfast, take a walk, take a nap, and get ready for his homecoming by being in a good mood and beautifully dressed. *Is this a joke?* I asked myself. *Did I marry a control freak?* I threw the note into the trash can and planned my day the way I wanted.

I knew Ida Mae would be arriving soon, but before she came, I wanted to start a routine of taking our puppy, Nutmeg, for a daily walk. The morning was warm and bright when I walked to Laura's to get the dog. As we set off down the paved driveway toward the highway, Nutmeg was happy, and his tail wagged nonstop as he stopped to sniff every rock and flower he passed. Then he took off running full speed through the fields of wild Queen Anne's lace. As we got closer to the road and I saw cars flying by, I called him, but instead of coming to me, he veered off toward the hangar. When I followed him, I was surprised to find tuxedo pieces—vests, cummerbunds, and bow ties—scattered in the grass around the landing strip. I wondered, *What on earth?* I picked them up to show Brad that evening and called Nutmeg.

On our return trip down the driveway, I admired the white split-rail fence that separated the grassy fields from the mowed lawn. I had never walked the grounds before, and I took my time to admire how lovely the white wooden house was with its black shutters and slate roof. I followed the circular drive to the front steps leading up to the large covered porch with Chippendale railing. As a designer and student of architecture, I was delighted to explore the details of the old plantation house in depth. The long, vertical first-floor windows still had their original glass. The front windows of the second floor were large dormers, while the basement windows were a little smaller and almost at ground level. The two large chimneys, one at either end of the house, had a hexfoil witches' mark. Nutmeg followed me as I went up the stairs and sat in one of the white wooden rocking chairs. Gazing out at the English boxwoods, huge magnolia trees, and azaleas in front of the house, I was enchanted by the beauty of the spacious landscape. I smiled with satisfaction and thought, *This elegant estate is now my home.*

Ida Mae arrived soon after I finished breakfast, and we made plans to organize the storage spaces in the house so that I would have room for my clothes and furniture. As we worked, I became more familiar with the inside of the house and made the decision to give the bedrooms upstairs first priority. I thought, *I need to make them comfortable before tackling the downstairs.* I was excited just thinking about the decorating possibilities and began making mental notes for how to best use my professional skills to get the house ready for entertaining.

I discovered I would need to replace all the entertaining supplies. When I looked puzzled about the lack of basic necessities, Ida Mae said, "Brad and Nancy divided everything equally when they got divorced, even dishes and place mats. So if a set had four items, they each got two." I didn't understand the reason for doing that, because neither of them ended up with much that was useful. It was the easy way out, I guessed.

Brad referred to everything as "ours" and gave me his permission to do whatever I wanted with the house. He hadn't had many repairs done over the years, so the place desperately needed work. With so much to do, my morning went by quickly but productively. I called for estimates on having central air-conditioning installed. I already knew that would be a hard sell to Brad because he didn't like air-conditioning. When he was at my house in Williamsburg, he wanted the doors left open, even when the AC was running. Since all of Riverwood's water came from a well, my second priority was to schedule a filtering system to be installed to improve the taste and smell of the water. I also scheduled an exterminator to get rid of the monster brown crickets jumping on the walls in the basement and the mice that occasionally scurried here and there.

As Ida Mae and I worked together that morning, I told her, "You'll have to be on your own this afternoon because I'll need time to cook a special meal and get ready for Brad before he gets home this evening." Ida Mae had been cooking and shopping for the family for many years, so she had seen that the kitchen was returned to full functioning status after Nancy had removed what she wanted. Ida Mae had always done a good job of keeping the refrigerator and freezer well stocked so she could be ready to cook dinner for the family's surprise guests and short-notice parties. Since she usually cooked dinner, she offered to help me, but I said, "Thanks, but this is something I want to do myself tonight."

By the time Brad was due home, I was wearing my new lavender silk sundress that had come by UPS that day. I was positive it would get a wow reaction from him when he walked in and saw me. It just so happened I had a pair of sandals that matched the dress.

I went downstairs to put the finishing touches on my gourmet dinner. As soon as I put it in the oven to stay warm, I heard Brad's plane coming in. I couldn't wait to tell him about the progress Ida Mae and I had made that day, but the most important thing to me was for him to experience the wonderful dinner I had prepared so he could discover what a good cook I was. I had high expectations of how my welcoming him home and hearing all about his day would go.

The house phone rang the moment I saw Brad's car coming down the driveway from the hangar. When he parked in front of the house, he paused to finish his cell phone call before coming inside. As he walked in the front door, before I could say a word to tell him how happy I was to see him, he took the phone from my hand and started talking without even saying hello to me. My mood deflated as he ignored my efforts for our first dinner at home and didn't even notice how I looked. While he was on the phone, I returned to the kitchen to do last-minute things to get dinner on the table. All sorts of thoughts were going through my head. One in particular was that I felt as if I were simply a replacement for Nancy. Since Brad had been married to her for so long, I was sure he was used to ignoring her when he came home. *Are my expectations too high in wanting him to acknowledge me when he gets home from work? What about all the time I spent fixing this fantastic dinner instead of serving him Ida Mae's casserole?*

While I was moping and feeling sorry for myself, Brad finished his phone call and headed upstairs to shower. He returned shortly to the dining room, smelling fresh and looking like a different person in his clean clothes. As we took our seats at the table, I told him I hoped our first at-home dinner as a married couple would be perfect and lead into a special evening, but his cell phone rang before I could finish my thought. Brad jumped up to go answer it and then sat down and carried on a phone conversation as he finished eating. Then he got up from the table. I followed him downstairs to the family room, where he turned on the TV to watch the evening news while still keeping the phone pressed to his ear. I sat down on the sofa as close to him as I could. When he finally hung up the phone, I asked, "Who were you talking to?"

"It was Martin—he forgot to tell me something when he called earlier."

As soon as the news program was over, Brad gathered up the letters, airplane magazines, and equipment auction newsletters that had arrived in the mail that day and took them upstairs to the bedroom. He liked to get ready for bed and then spread the mail out on the bed to go through it. He had all the business mail sent directly to the house so he could be the first to read it in order to keep up with money coming into the company and money owed. After that, he could relax with magazines and newsletters.

I headed to the kitchen to clean up and load the dishwasher. When I went upstairs with a glass of wine to join Brad, he was already asleep. I wasn't surprised because he had looked tired when he got home. He also had been away from his work for more than a week, so I knew he had a lot to catch up on. I went to the bedroom I had claimed as my dressing room to read until I was sleepy enough to join him. I was a little disappointed that the evening hadn't turn out as I had hoped, but I reminded myself that Brad carried a big responsibility on his shoulders in running such a large business. *Look how well he provides for me*, I thought.

Chapter 19

As that first week went by, I finally realized that as soon as Brad came home, phone calls would be an everyday occurrence. I was always going to be standing there impatiently tapping my fingers, waiting to hand him the phone when he walked through the door. But Friday was a happy exception—he came home, showered, and dressed in a sports coat and tie to take me out for drinks and dinner. He was back to treating me like a princess, the way he had in our dating days. He made sure we sat close to each other so he could hold my hand during the meal. The restaurant we went to had someone playing the piano, so a few couples, including us, got up and danced. When I returned from going to the ladies' room, Brad stood up to greet me with open arms and pull out my chair for me. He made me feel that he was happy to be with me.

But the next morning, he was off to work again. When we were dating, he often had checked on a few of his working projects on Saturdays. I had even gone with him sometimes, so I wasn't surprised when he got up and left home early that first Saturday. When he returned home around two o'clock that afternoon, he had flowers and a hug for me.

"They're beautiful, Brad," I said. "Thank you for thinking of me."

That evening, as I was dressing for our night out, Brad brought me a glass of wine before he went into the bedroom to dress for the evening. When he returned, I was putting the final touches on my hair. He walked up behind me, put his hands around my waist, and then bent to press kisses onto my neck. Raising his head, he captured my eyes in the mirror and said huskily, "You look incredibly sexy tonight." He unzipped the back of my dress and slid it down over my shoulders, and we ended up making love before going out.

We went to dinner at the local country club. I loved going to the club because I could dress up in my evening wear. He made sure we were home by ten o'clock because we were going to church in the morning, as we had done throughout our courtship, even when away on vacation.

The next morning, Brad brought me a cup of coffee to drink while I was dressing for church, impressing me with his thoughtfulness. He also gave his approval of the outfit I had selected, telling me, "You look so good you might cause the reverend to forget his sermon."

We were attending our church for the first time as a married couple, and we received many good wishes from members of the congregation. When we stopped for lunch on the way home, Brad told me he wanted to go see his dad that afternoon. After our visit with him, we stopped to have a light dinner. As soon as we got home, Brad started planning his work schedule for the next week. He said the friend who used to own his business had told him many times, "To be successful, you need to spend Sunday evenings preparing for the coming work week."

"I took his advice to heart," Brad said. "So I've always been ready to go on Monday mornings."

That first week set the pattern for my new life. When Brad arrived home every workday, I noticed that his first caller was usually Martin, who apparently entertained himself during his boring commute home by telling his dad about what had happened at work that day. Since the calls interfered with our dinner hour and made Brad late for dinner, I suggested he ask Martin to call later. He refused because he didn't want to disrupt Martin's routine. Brad accused me of not wanting him to call and said, "You don't like Martin."

I was disturbed that Brad was so concerned about Martin and not at all concerned about me. I tried explaining, saying, "It's not that I don't like Martin, Brad. I just don't want our dinner to be disrupted every night, especially since you want it served in the dining room and want us to be well dressed."

Brad often invited Martin to dinner at the last minute on days when I only had enough food prepared for the two of us.

"Brad," I said, "please let me know ahead of time before you invite him so there'll be enough food for all of us."

"Martin can have my food," he snapped. "You don't like my children." I was bewildered that he would make such an outrageous statement.

Our weeknights continued to have the same routine, and I realized that our home was just another business office and that Brad wasn't interested in me while he was conducting business. Sometimes I overheard him encouraging his employees to buy expensive things and overextend themselves financially. It became more and more evident to me how he manipulated people with his power of persuasion to get and keep control of them. I saw that the more dependent on him he could make people, the more control their dependence gave him over them. After he finished eating dinner, his bedtime routine stayed the same night after night during the week, so he could be asleep by nine o'clock.

I worked hard the first two weeks to get our private rooms upstairs decorated to my liking. Our large master bedroom had a fireplace with a brick hearth and wooden mantel, so I envisioned that when the weather got colder, we would snuggle in front of a warm, cozy fire. To that end, I placed an inviting bearskin rug between two comfortable armchairs and the fireplace. I replaced the old wooden double bed with an antique queen-size brass bed and added a custom-made bedspread in a red flowered print with matching draperies. Antique cherry bedside tables and chests completed the room. We also had a large bathroom and walk-in closet.

On the landing were another bathroom and more storage closets, with a smaller bedroom on the other side. I put a small antique bed in that room so it could be used as needed for guests. Mostly, I used it as my dressing room and decorated it appropriately with a full-length mirror, a chest, and a pink velvet chaise lounge next to a small table with a brass pharmacy lamp and telephone. That bedroom also had a fireplace with brick hearth and wooden mantel. After Brad went to sleep, I spent my evenings there, reading until I was sleepy enough to go to bed too. He was unhappy that I didn't go to sleep when he did. Many nights, he would get out of bed, annoyed, and come into the room where I was reading to ask, "Why don't you come to bed?"

"Brad, for the umpteenth time, I can't go to sleep this early," I would answer.

Some nights, just to keep the peace, I went to bed early with him, only to lie there staring at the ceiling. Other nights, I tried to compromise by getting into bed to make love and then getting back up to read until I got sleepy. Doing that was still not good enough. My bedtime hour quickly escalated into an ongoing disagreement. I couldn't understand why he didn't appreciate that I never complained about my lonely evenings without him because he went to bed so early. I kept remembering how we had stayed up talking till all hours of the night before we got married. *What happened to that?*

He continued to leave me daily notes. I finally said, "Brad, I think the notes you're leaving me are ridiculous. I don't need you to plan my day." His reaction was to stomp out of the room, so it was evident he didn't like my independent side. *How did I miss his controlling ways all this time?*

I had also gotten my own furniture and most of my belongings moved into Riverwood. I had sold my house in Williamsburg, so I drove down to get the last of my things before the new owners moved in. Brad was working at a job site in Richmond, so he wanted me to drive there and spend the night with him in a motel when I finished in Williamsburg. After packing and loading the car with the last items, I did a thorough cleaning of the whole house. When I finished, it was late, and I was so exhausted that I decided to spend the night at a motel in Williamsburg instead of driving to Richmond. When I called to tell Brad about my decision, he wasn't happy and let me know it. He questioned me. "Why are you staying in Williamsburg? That wasn't our plan." It didn't seem to matter to him that I was tired and hungry, and nothing I said made him understand my reasons for not wanting to drive sixty miles late at night. After we'd argued on the phone for a good while, I finally said good night. I wasn't sure, but I thought he might have hung up on me.

The next morning, I got up early and drove back to Riverwood, ready to continue my new life. After Ida Mae helped me unload the car and put things away, I prepared a nice dinner and dressed in bright yellow shorts with a matching top, one of Brad's favorite outfits. I hoped he was over our last night's misunderstanding. I couldn't believe we had already had a big argument that early in our marriage.

When he came in the door, I could tell by the scornful look on his face that he was still unhappy. He slammed his briefcase down on the dining room table, pulled out a notepad, and looked at it before berating me for all the bad things I had done thus far. I was astonished to realize he had made a list of my so-called infractions: I didn't get up when he got up, I didn't follow his day-planner instructions, I didn't like his children, and I stayed up late.

I refused to argue with Brad because I knew I couldn't win any of his arguing points, so I left the room and went upstairs to my dressing room. Shortly afterward, he appeared with a glass of wine for me, smiling and acting as if we had never argued. He stroked my leg and said, "You look so beautiful in those sexy yellow shorts." I was bewildered at how fast he had changed moods.

One day during those first weeks of marriage, I got an anonymous letter that made several accusations about Brad's being unfaithful and dishonest. It said if I wanted more information to write to a post office box in Raleigh, North Carolina, where he had once owned a plant. I didn't respond to the letter because I was trying to get our marriage off to a good start and had no way of knowing if the information about his possible dishonorable behavior were real or not. I didn't want to upset Brad, so I waited until Saturday evening, when we were relaxing on the side porch, to show him the letter. He blew it off. "Oh, that could be from my ex-wife. You know she's jealous that you and I have such an excellent relationship."

Chapter 20

By the first of July, Brad no longer left a to-do list for me every morning, but he still wrote notes telling me how he wanted me to be dressed when he got home. All the notes were good, such as, "Husband likes your beautiful clothes." I had unlimited buying power when it came to new clothes because he wanted me to look like a model all the time. After I had worn something for only a short while, he'd tell me, "I've seen that outfit. Go put something else on." In fact, I changed clothes so often that it was tiring. He also preferred I go braless most of the time and wear see-through blouses and short skirts. His attitude toward boudoir clothing was "The skimpier the better." I enjoyed dressing provocatively for him when we were home alone and seeing his response when he looked at me. However, he also had a habit of buying me clothes that weren't appropriate for wearing in public and then insisting I wear them anyway, even though I wasn't comfortable doing so.

"Brad," I told him patiently, "you know I'll wear anything you want me to at home, but I refuse to wear clothing that isn't suitable outside the home. I do not wear hot pants and extremely short skirts in public. People would look at me like I've lost my mind." Our fighting about the issue lessened when I started putting together several more appropriate outfits and asking him to pick the one he wanted me to wear.

Another thing I soon learned was not to tell Brad I was going to get a haircut. He wanted my hair long, and when I said the word *haircut*, he assumed my hair would be short when I got back home. I learned to avoid an argument by saying, "I'm going to get my hair trimmed."

He also wasn't happy if I had my fingernails painted any color but red. I mostly obliged him with that request. He repeatedly told me, "I want your hands to look nice, not like hands that work."

In addition to my learning to live with Brad, country life was proving to be different from the city lifestyle I had always been used to. I was mostly isolated at Riverwood because no one lived within sight except Laura and Martin. However, being the household social planner helped keep me busy and in contact with people. A few of the local ladies visited me to welcome me to the community and ask if I would be interested in joining a bridge club or helping with charity organizations.

I liked taking Nutmeg for daily walks because it got me out into nature and gave me time to think about projects that still needed to be done to the house. He liked to go down by the river and through the fields where our neighbor's cows grazed. I had to be careful to step around giant cow patties as I tried to keep up with him. The cows often knocked down the fence and wandered over to enjoy the grass in our front yard, and it was always a surprise to glance out the window and see a herd of cows in my yard. Even more surprising was when I sometimes saw huge black snakes basking in the hot summer sun on the fence rails. Sometimes one would even be hanging from a tree limb.

One morning, I went out onto the back porch, where the dog's bowls were located, and found an unfamiliar animal curled around a bowl. Nutmeg pawed at it, but the animal wouldn't let go. I got a broom so I could poke it without getting too close, but it still wouldn't budge. Ida Mae suggested I call animal control for advice. Being a city girl, I would never have thought of calling them. They told me it was a possum, and if I left it alone, it would go away. So that was what I did, and it left when I wasn't looking. Although I still didn't really know what a possum looked like, I'd learned what playing possum meant.

Right after the possum visit, I went shopping and left Ida Mae doing laundry while a painter worked on the outside of the house. He removed the screens from the basement windows, which were only a few inches off the ground, and left the windows open to dry. A fox went into the house through an open window and lay down on one of my sweaters that was spread out to dry on the utility room counter. Ida Mae found the fox and called animal control. By the time they arrived, the fox had gone back outside and headed toward a shed. They determined the fox was rabid, so they had to shoot him. When Ida Mae told me about the fox lying on one of my favorite sweaters, I exclaimed, "Oh no, that was the sweater I got as a souvenir from our trip to Sanibel Island, Florida! Now I'll have to throw it away."

The next morning, while the screens were still out, I was awakened by something pecking on my ear. *It's Brad being romantic*, I thought, smiling. It took me a few moments to figure out it wasn't Brad causing the strange sensation—it was a bird! I swatted the bird away and chased it as it flew frantically around the room before finally flying out the window.

In mid-July, the weather turned hot and excruciatingly humid. I was uncomfortable with my clothes sticking to me, so I was glad when the day finally came for the AC to be installed. Brad, however, wasn't happy with the placement of the outside unit and wanted it moved to another location regardless of the extra labor involved. He was rude and demanding to the installers, which was embarrassing to me since I had been the one working with the company from the beginning. Finally, though, the unit was up and running. I had never lived without air-conditioning, so I was happy to be comfortable again.

Toward the end of July, when I told Brad that my sister,

Shirley, was going with her husband, Jimmy, to Charleston while he attended a business conference, he volunteered to fly me there to keep her company. He even suggested we stop by Wilmington to pick up my mother, who was enormously impressed with the generosity of her new son-in-law.

While I was shopping with my mother and sister in Charleston, a jewelry store caught my attention, so I decided to look at their wedding rings. Almost immediately, I spotted the perfect ring to replace my solid gold band. The two rows of diamonds on the band beautifully matched my large diamond solitaire ring. I hurried back to the hotel and told Brad, "You have to come see a ring I found. I want it to be my wedding band." When he saw it, Brad agreed that I had at last found the perfect ring. He pulled out his credit card, and I became the proud owner of the ring. My mother was impressed again with Brad's generosity in buying the ring I wanted.

While we were in Charleston, Mother told me she thought I should know about the wild drug party at the airplane hangar after Brad and I left the wedding reception. In the middle of the night, they had been awakened by speeding cars roaring up and down the concrete runway. By the time Jimmy had gone out to investigate, the cars were parked at the hangar, and he could see people inside. Graham came out and told him not to come any closer, but Jimmy was already close enough to see that Martin and Laura were inside, and all three of them appeared to be high on drugs. "Well," I said, "I guess that explains the clothing I found strewn around the yard after we got home from our honeymoon."

Chapter 21

AUGUST TO SEPTEMBER, YEAR TWO
RIVERWOOD ESTATE

In August, when I had our private rooms upstairs comfortable, I turned my attention to the public rooms downstairs. I wanted our guests to enjoy the beautiful house from the moment they stepped through the massive front door. I began by measuring the downstairs rooms and drawing them to scale to help with my furniture purchases and placement. My next task was to decide what furniture I needed, so with notebook in hand, I stood with my back to the front door and tried to look at the rooms as if I were seeing them for the first time.

I immediately noticed the large crystal chandelier that hung from the twelve-foot ceiling and sent sparkles of light to every surface. To the left was the vast doorway to the living room, and I could see the fireplace and mantel on the far wall. *Something special needs to go there*, I thought. Next to that door were the wide wooden stairs going up to a balcony that traversed the whole foyer from the left wall to the right, where another set of steps continued up to the second floor. *The walls beside the steps and behind the balcony will be perfect for an impressive art gallery,* I thought. Directly in front of me below the balcony was a door leading to the back hall. A door to the left led to a half bath under the stairs, and a door to the right led to the basement. *Hmm*, I thought. *A grandfather clock, a love seat, and a sideboard will do nicely here in the foyer.*

Turning to the right and looking through the doorway of the dining room, I saw a blank wall, so I made a note that an eye-catching work of art should be there for a visitor to see from the door. Stepping away from the front door and turning around, I saw that the wide windows on either side of the door didn't need drapery; just swags would suffice. The warmth of the wooden moldings and wainscoting cried out for a soft palette. *Creams and subdued colors*, I thought. *And an antique Persian rug on these old plank floors will be perfect too.*

Satisfied that the foyer would impress, I paused at the doorway to the living room. The room ran almost the full depth of the house, so I immediately knew I would have two seating areas: one in front of the fireplace and one near the front windows. I envisioned an off-white Chippendale sofa flanked by small blue Sheraton chairs, cherry end tables and tea table for the fireplace area, and an off-white Queen Anne wing chair with a round cherry side table for the front of the room. A secretary and two chests, also in cherry, would fill in the remaining gaps around the room.

I then turned my attention to the inside wall lined with built-in bookcases partially filled with old books that had belonged to the previous owner. I could visualize adding my books, small accessories, and family photos to finish filling out the shelves. The paneled fireplace mantel and floor-to-ceiling surround was painted Williamsburg cream, as were the crown molding, baseboard, and wainscoting around the room. The walls were painted the same color but a shade lighter. Two globed sconces, each holding two candles, were on either side of the surround just above the mantel. I decided the windows should have floor-length silk draperies and cornice boards that were a slightly darker cream than the walls, but the French door to the side porch could be left uncovered. An oversize oriental rug, large pictures, lamps, a huge ficus tree, and various accessories would complete the room.

When I was pleased with my plan for the living room, I turned to the dining room. It too was a large room. It comfortably held an oval table with twelve Chippendale chairs, which—along with two huge silver candelabras—had come with the house. The room had the same stained wooden wainscoting and crown molding that were in the entrance foyer, and the walls were painted the same cream as the living room. I noted I would need another oriental rug to cover the plank floor. The window draperies would match those in the living room. The fireplace mantel and surround were identical to those of the living room, except they were stained instead of painted. Since the ceiling was so high, huge pictures with ornate frames would fit on the walls nicely. The oversize crystal chandelier hanging over the table was gorgeous. The only furniture I needed to add there were a corner china cabinet and a chest.

Moving to the butler's pantry between the dining room and the kitchen, I admired the floor-to-ceiling cabinets that took up one whole wall. They were mostly empty, and I mused over what I needed to fill them. Another wall had counter space with upper cabinets, as did the outside wall, with upper cabinets on either side of a window.

As I entered the remodeled kitchen and looked around, I appreciated that the double ovens would be an asset for entertaining, as would the Jenn-Air range, extra-large refrigerator, and plenty of cabinets and counter space. A walk-in pantry was near the back door that led to the small porch overlooking the tennis courts. Looking out at the backyard, I marveled at the open space and view of the river in the distance. Turning to the kitchen sink window, I could see out to the guesthouse and Brad's grass airplane runway. The small wooden table flanked by two chairs in the center of the room was cozy for breakfast and lunch and was also useful as extra counter space when preparing meals.

A long hall led from the kitchen all the way across the length of the house to the side porch, which butted up to the rear wall of the living room. Stepping into the hall, I noted that the door to the left led to the foyer, and the door to the right opened into a large guest bedroom with a full bathroom and double windows that overlooked the pool. For that room, I decided on a queen-sized four-poster cherry bed with matching custom-made bedspread and swag draperies.

I knew I had to work fast to get the house ready for the Thanksgiving and Christmas holidays. Later that week, Brad and I flew to Wilson, North Carolina, where Boone's Antiques, a contact I had from my interior design business, was located. They had a huge warehouse full of beautiful wooden furniture in excellent condition. Since I knew exactly what I needed, it didn't take long for me to find everything on my list.

I just needed the upholstered pieces, draperies, pictures, lamps, and other accessories, so it was time to visit my old design store in Williamsburg. I was sure Martha would welcome my business and expedite the orders so I could have the house ready by Thanksgiving.

A few weeks later, Martha came to visit to see how I was progressing with my decorating. That evening, she and I went out to dinner and a play. It was close to midnight when we arrived back home to find that Brad had locked the door and turned out all the lights. On that cloudy, moonless night, it was dark and eerie there in the country. I banged on the door, and he finally came to let us in. He looked as if he had just woken up, and when I showed Martha to the guest room, we realized he had been sleeping in her bed. I was embarrassed and apologized to Martha for Brad's obvious misunderstanding about her spending the night. Since her bed in the guest room had been disturbed, I showed her to the bed in my dressing room.

Chapter 22

As summer moved into fall and the air turned chilly, Brad told me he had arranged for Graham to drive me to the same store where I had gotten my full-length mink coat because he wanted me to pick out a mink jacket. I protested. "But I already have a mink coat."

"With the holidays coming up," he replied, "we'll be invited to lots of parties and social events. There'll be times when a short mink coat will be more appropriate than a long one, and I want my bride looking good." I happily obeyed and selected my new coat in the same black color as my full-length coat. It was lavish, comfy, and warm.

That evening, when Brad walked into the house, I greeted him wearing my new mink jacket with nothing else on underneath and gave him a preview flash as I handed him the phone. He was so taken aback that he stammered as he answered the call. Although he continued talking, I knew he was still looking at me as I ran upstairs to get dressed for dinner. At bedtime, Brad told me I should give him more surprises like that and insisted I come to bed with him.

When the leaves turned orange and gold, Brad took me for a sightseeing ride in the Cherokee. It was the first time I had ever flown so low to the ground, just over the treetops, and it was a remarkable way to see how beautiful the fall colors were. We stopped at Massanutten Ski Resort for lunch. Afterward, we took the riding ski lift to the top of the mountain to look around. Since it was early in the season, there was no snow yet. I told Brad, "Let's come back for a weekend vacation and ski the slopes. I know how to water-ski. Does that mean I can snow-ski too?"

"I think you'll find that there's a big difference, sweetheart," said Brad. "It's much more entertaining and safer to sit by the fire in the ski lodge while having drinks and watching other people ski. You're the social planner, so schedule a weekend for us to come back here when the season opens."

By November, I had completed my decorating plan for the downstairs. As I stood in the foyer and looked around, I was proud of my accomplishment in creating such warm and inviting rooms for our guests. I thought about how happy I was to be living in such a beautiful house made even more beautiful through my hard work. My design experience had been put to good use in that old plantation home, for I had fulfilled every designer's dream of having an unlimited budget to decorate a house inside and out. I looked forward to having our families gather at our home for a Thanksgiving feast, which I hoped would become a tradition. With the decorating complete, my thoughts turned to planning the meal.

Early Thanksgiving morning, Brad flew down to Wilmington and picked up my mother, Elizabeth, and her sister, Sally, who had come with her husband, Calvin, from Michigan to spend Thanksgiving with my mother and would stay in the Riverwood guesthouse. We'd also invited Martin and his girlfriend, Addison, as well as Laura; her husband, Sam; and Dawn. Brad's mother, Vivian, and dad, William, also had been invited, even though Brad and I had disagreed about inviting his mother. He'd said she would just spoil the day, but I couldn't in good conscience exclude her.

I made a large wreath with fall flowers for the front door and placed pots of yellow and orange mums on the front porch and steps. I had worked for days to prepare the huge buffet and set the table correctly. I made a cornucopia with a horn-shaped wicker basket filled with small pumpkins, corn husks, and different types of squash, and I put burnt-orange candles in the candelabras on the table. We would have turkey, ham, and so many vegetable dishes and desserts that I knew our guests would have a hard time deciding what to choose.

After everyone was seated at the table, I told them how happy Brad and I were to have both our families with us to celebrate our first Thanksgiving as a married couple. Aunt Sally kindly made a toast to our generosity and my fine job of serving such a bountiful Thanksgiving meal and decorating the house so beautifully since she had last seen it on our wedding day.

"You must have worked night and day to get it looking so festive," she said.

"This house does consume most of my time," I said.

When the holiday weekend was over, I went with Brad to fly my family back home. We ran into rough weather, so he decided we should land in Jacksonville, North Carolina, instead of continuing to Wilmington. I knew he was always a cautious pilot, so I trusted his decision to keep us safe. The Gulfstream we were flying that day had sophisticated instrumentation. Brad had an instrument rating, so he knew how to navigate in darkness or bad weather. He kept his skill current by practicing touch-and-go in inclement weather and always kept the planes maintained on schedule. After flying with Brad so many times, I was confident in his ability to handle any situation.

When we landed, Mother called my cousin Frank and asked him to come pick them up and drive them the rest of the way home. Aunt Sally kept saying, "We could have died." I assured her we had not been in any danger of dying.

I shared with her a story about when I'd been concerned about the safety of the plane on a trip back home last February. We'd been returning home from Fort Walton Beach, Florida, when suddenly, all the cockpit panel lights had come on at the same time. I always sat in the copilot seat when we flew alone, so I immediately had seen that there was a problem. We'd stopped in Wilmington so Brad could get the plane checked out, but they'd been unable to find any reason for the lights to be on. I had still been uncomfortable about continuing the flight home and annoyed with Brad for not comforting me when I was obviously worried. He'd kept telling me I was overreacting and saying there was nothing to worry about. I finally had asked the maintenance guy if he would fly the plane under those conditions, and he'd said he would, so I'd felt reassured as we continued the trip back to Charlottesville General Aviation, where Brad had left the aircraft for repair and maintenance. I had since learned to trust his judgment, and I knew Brad wouldn't fly if he thought he would be putting himself or his passengers in any danger.

As soon as Brad and I got back into the air headed home, he said, "We need to start making our Christmas party plans."

"You want to have a Christmas party?" I said in surprise.

"Yes, I do," said Brad. "You have done such an exceptional job of redoing our house that we need to show it off. If I know you, Princess, when you decorate the house for Christmas, it'll be something to see. We need our party to be the first party of the season because people get burned out close to Christmas."

"All right then," I replied. "I'll get right to work on the menu and decorating. We need to make a list of people to invite too."

Our Eleuthera friends, Brenda and Joe, were one of the first couples I thought of. We had visited them at their Topsail Beach home often that past summer on our way to and from Wilmington. They, in turn, had joined us at Riverwood for most of our summer get-togethers, telling us how much they enjoyed spending time in the country away from all the beach traffic and tourists. Then, to my surprise, Brad added Paula Simon, an acquaintance from our church, to the top of the invitation list. I wondered why she was the first person Brad thought of to invite, but I didn't ask. As we kept working on the invitation list, we added the reverend and several other couples from church. The list kept growing as we added people we knew from the community as well as a few of Brad's business associates. Brad and I agreed that twenty couples would be a nice-sized group, but trying to keep the guest list that short was a challenge.

"Brad," I said, laughing, "you and I just know too many people."

Our first Christmas party at Riverwood was small compared to other parties we had attended since being married. Ida Mae and I did all the food preparation. We had a ham at one end of the dining room table and a turkey at the other end. We also had the usual party dishes of meatballs, fruit, and a veggie tray. The variety of desserts Ida Mae made were so good that they looked and tasted as if they had jumped right out of a *Southern Living* cookbook. I used my floral expertise to create a large centerpiece with holly and poinsettias. We hired a professional bartender because neither Brad nor I wanted to be tied up tending bar.

The long bannister rail on the balcony overlooking the entrance foyer was perfect for decorating with Christmas greenery, and I put a large Christmas tree beside the front door. Judging from all the compliments we received about the food and how festive the house looked, the party was a success. Our guests stayed so late mingling and drinking, obviously enjoying themselves, that Brad and I began to think they were going to spend the night with us.

After our party, we looked forward to attending other parties. Riley and Hannah, a couple from church, invited us to their huge Christmas Eve party. Close to midnight, the party ended with all the guests driving to our nearby church to attend the Christmas Eve service. Brad and I drove in the new Mercedes he had given me as my Christmas gift. The car had been delivered that day with a huge red ribbon tied on top.

"Oh, Brad!" I'd exclaimed as I threw my arms around his neck. "Yet another surprise for me. How will I ever be able to thank you?"

Christmas Day at Riverwood was quiet for Brad and me. The

day was warm, so we put Nutmeg in the backseat of the Cherokee and took off with no place in mind. We flew all around the area, enjoying the scenery. Nutmeg seemed to enjoy his first airplane ride.

On New Year's Eve, we went to the Greenbrier Resort in West Virginia, where we had spent a few days of our honeymoon. Fresh snow continued to fall after we landed at the airport, adding to the snow already on the ground. When we drove up to the entrance, I exclaimed, "Oh my, I've never seen a place so beautifully decorated!" All the windows had large wreaths with red bows, and every bush and tree was covered with white lights twinkling through the snow. When we entered the large foyer, my breath was taken away by the myriads of poinsettias surrounding huge ice sculptures of a Christmas tree, snowman, and sleigh.

After we got settled in our room, Brad said, "I have a surprise for you outside, sweetheart, so put on your full-length mink and those snow boots I told you to pack." Grinning, he led me out to a holly-bedecked sleigh behind a horse with jingle bells around its neck. I was delighted when I saw his surprise. When we got into the sleigh, we covered up with blankets, and off we went. Our driver was so jolly that I could tell he enjoyed his job. He was even singing "Jingle Bells." The sleigh ride was so much fun that I couldn't stop laughing. I had always dreamed about cuddling in a sleigh on a cold winter's night and going dashing through the snow.

"Brad, how did you know this was on my bucket list of things to do?"

"Don't you remember that I have psychic abilities when it comes to knowing what you like?"

"I've never had so much fun. Thank you for this amazing experience," I said, snuggling closer to him. "I can't wait for your next surprise."

When the ride was over and we got out of the sleigh, Brad reached down to make a snowball and throw it at me.

"Okay, Mr. Brad, does this mean you want a snowball fight?"

Giggling like teenagers, we threw a few snowballs back and forth at each other on our way inside.

As the eight o'clock hour got closer, I dressed in my floor-length, long-sleeved, off-the-shoulders black velvet dress, which was form-fitting to my knees before flaring out. *This is great for dancing*, I thought as I twirled around in anticipation. A cameo on a black velvet ribbon around my neck pulled my outfit together. While Brad was getting dressed, he caught a glimpse of me in the mirror. He turned around, took me in his arms, and said, "You look so good. Let's skip the party, stay in our room, and make love."

"Later, Brad," I replied with a smirk. "There's dancing to be done first."

The ballroom where we dined and danced was a magical fairyland with enormous crystal chandeliers. The dining tables had glowing candles and sprigs of holly. The band was great, and I was captivated by the music and magic of the atmosphere.

At about ten o'clock, Brad suddenly stood up and said, "I've had enough. Let's go."

"Oh no!" I protested. "I'm having a perfect time. I don't want to leave." But my feelings didn't matter to him. He only glared at me as he turned and walked away. I reluctantly gathered my purse and tried to watch the band over my shoulder as I slowly followed him out of the ballroom. Brad stomped down the hallway ahead of me to our hotel room. I was disappointed and upset that he'd disregarded my wish to stay until the ball dropped at midnight. I sadly thought, *He'll probably add this to his list of things he doesn't like.*

Back in the room, he went to bed immediately without even saying good night. I slowly undressed, got ready for bed, and then sat in the dark for what seemed like hours, wondering what had gone wrong.

The next morning, New Year's Day, Brad was still sullen, and we left right after breakfast. On the flight home, I remained quiet but kept questioning in my mind why he would spend so much money and then not enjoy the evening. It seemed to me that he didn't know how to stay in one place for long.

When we got home, Brad's mood changed completely. He seemed more relaxed as he took a beer out of the refrigerator and built a fire in the oversize fireplace in our cozy basement family room, one of my favorite rooms in the house. It had hand-hewn beams overhead, and the floor was made of brick. As we settled down on the couch for a quiet day of reading and being on the computer, I sent email wishes for a happy and prosperous new year to my family and all our friends. Brad spent some time in the office next to the family room to write down work ideas for the coming year. The children popped in to wish us a happy New Year on their way out and about. Nutmeg kept us company and enjoyed sleeping on his bed by the fire.

As the day came to an end, I sat down next to Brad on the sofa and reached for his hand. He turned, looked at me thoughtfully, and said, "You always like sitting close to me." Then he leaned over to give me a kiss and said, "Happy New Year, Princess. I'm looking forward to having another wonderful year together." Then he stood and pulled me to my feet. "C'mon. It's nine o'clock. Let's call it a day."

Chapter 23

After the holidays, we decided to beat the cold and monotonous weather by going to Key Colony, Florida, for the month of January. We rented a house near the Marathon Airport, where we rented a car and left the airplane so that Brad could easily leave and return in the event of a business emergency. Key West wasn't far away, so we often went there to Sloppy Joe's for food and music. While we were in Key West, Brad usually insisted we go shopping to buy something special for me and get a key lime pie to take back to the house with us. We enjoyed our stay at Key Colony so much that we agreed we should go there every year, so Brad told the rental agent to sign us up for next January.

Despite our ongoing disagreements, I did not doubt that Brad loved me. He continued to send me roses at home often. He loved to give me surprises and to be surprised himself. He often brought a gift home to me at the end of his workday. Sometimes for no reason at all, he would give me a corsage to wear to church, and he always made sure I had a glass of wine to drink while getting dressed to go out in the evening. He knew how to behave like a real southern gentleman—but not the time we were at the Kentucky Derby.

As a little girl, I'd loved to watch the Kentucky Derby races on

TV every May with my father. I'd been mesmerized by the beauty of the horses and kept telling him, "I want a horse like that."

My father would answer, "I do too."

Brad knew my Kentucky Derby history, so as a gift for our first wedding anniversary, he surprised me by asking, "Why don't we go to the derby this year?"

"Oh, Brad," I happily responded. "That's one of the most thoughtful things I've ever heard you say. Can we really go to the Kentucky Derby?"

Our trip there started out as great fun. When we arrived at the airport in Louisville, the airport runway attendant instructed us to park our plane. After securing our aircraft, we looked for a ride to Churchill Downs, where the race would take place. As luck would have it, an idle limo driver volunteered to take us there. When our stretch limo arrived at the front entrance, people in the crowd pressed forward and gawked at us, hoping to see celebrities. When the chauffeur opened the car door for me to take his hand and step out, I couldn't conceal my long legs, high heels, and short dress. Of course, I had to act the part of being someone famous, so I kept my hat tipped down so that my long blonde hair fell forward to hide my face. As Brad offered his arm to me, the smiling crowd parted for us, and we walked through them like royalty.

On the way to our reserved box seats, we stopped to get mint juleps. As we sipped our drinks, Brad looked over my hot-pink sundress and said, "You look gorgeous, Princess. That short skirt does a good job of showing off your perfect legs. I like your sexy hat too." I flushed with pleasure, pleased that he liked the floral hat I had ordered from a famous hat maker in Kentucky.

When we sat down, my seat happened to be next to a nice-looking man who smiled and complimented me on my hat. "Is this your first time at the derby?" he asked.

"Yes," I said. "But I'm one of its biggest fans. I've always made sure I was near a TV during the race. What about you? Have you been here before?"

"Oh yes, many times. I wouldn't miss this event for the world."

When my neighbor continued to keep me engaged in conversation, Brad suddenly stood up and said, "Come with me." After getting us more mint juleps, he refused to go back to our seats. Instead, we wandered around in the crowd and missed the race we had come to see, all because of Brad's jealousy.

When there wasn't any discord in our relationship and I snuggled up to Brad's back in bed at night, I felt a current running between us that gave me a sense of peace, but when he went on a tangent, that current disappeared, and I felt nothing but emptiness. That happened on the warm June night we attended a debutante ball. On the way there, I told him about a problem I was having with the pool house contractor. He became outraged, gripping the steering wheel and gritting his teeth. "Just shut up! All you do is complain, and I don't want to hear it."

I didn't want the situation to escalate into a full-fledged fight, so I kept quiet. When Brad parked and got out of the car, he kicked the car door closed so hard that he put a dent in it. However, as we entered the ballroom and greeted everyone, I was surprised at how quickly his mood changed to being calm and relaxed. During the evening, friends even commented to me on the loving and sexy way he acted toward me. While we were dancing, Brad whispered in my ear how beautiful I looked in my green jewel-toned slip dress and how my rhinestone barrette was reflected in the shininess of my hair. He also made sure my wine glass stayed full. *He's back to being the perfect southern gentleman*, I thought.

Brad loved attending and giving parties, so we had many events my first year at Riverwood, from cookouts and formal dinner parties to oyster roasts on the tennis court area. I soon became known as a good cook and hostess. However, no matter how much entertaining we did, Brad irrationally accused me of not having parties. I tried to defend myself by reminding him of all I had done, but that only led to more arguing. Nothing I said changed his mind, and he added the lack of parties to his notepad list of my misdeeds.

His list of what I did or didn't do grew longer, so our arguments were also longer because he always started at the top of the list and worked his way down through all the items. That meant I had to reargue every argument I had ever had with him all over again every time. Finally, I figured out I was never going to win an argument with him. I became more and more aggravated and angry over how stupid I thought the situation was, so I tried to keep my lips tight and take deep breaths to keep myself calm. I wasn't sure if his memory was the problem or not, but we definitely had a communication problem. Brad did not always understand what I said and often misinterpreted my statements. I felt I was constantly saying, "But that's not what I said."

Occasionally, we would have heart-to-heart discussions that ended in complete agreement on what we were going to do to improve our relationship. Then, sometimes within minutes, Brad would do the exact thing we had just decided not to do. I would get frustrated because I couldn't understand why he would do that to me. I thought, *How can he be so thoughtful one minute and so mean to me the next? Living with Brad is like living with Dr. Jekyll and Mr. Hyde.*

Chapter 24

JUNE TO JANUARY, YEAR THREE
RIVERWOOD ESTATE

As the weather got warmer, Brad and I often enjoyed relaxing before dinner with drinks on the side porch. Sometimes we ate at the glass-topped table while watching the evening news on the porch TV. The location was perfect for lunches and entertaining because it was right down the hall from the kitchen. When my mother visited, she loved to sit on the porch and look out across the fields.

"This is my favorite spot in the house," she said. "The view is so serene and beautiful. If I lived here, I would sit out here forever."

The pool was another popular place to relax on warm evenings and weekends. The newly restored pool house with bar and bathroom gave swimmers a place to change, freshen up, and enjoy a snack or drink. One of my jobs was to keep the pool clean and the chemicals balanced. Many people complimented me on how clean I kept the pool. One time, I was brushing the bottom, when I reached too far and fell into the pool fully dressed, including my jewelry. When I returned to the main house, Ida Mae asked me if I had fallen into the pool. Feeling a bit foolish, I said, "No, I jumped in," and I headed upstairs to dry off and redress.

As I had moved through the first and second years of living at Riverwood, I had gradually acquired a circle of girlfriends to visit and go places with. That summer, I enjoyed having them join me for lunches and wine by the pool. Of course, I would be excited about having friends visit and would tell Brad about my plans. Several times, when I invited someone over, he came home, drove his car up close to the pool, and sat there with the car running. We would wave to him and keep floating on the pool loungers and talking to each other. I would think to myself, *I wonder why he's home during the workday?*

That September, I thought it would be fun to take a creative writing class at the local college. One day while class was in session, I was surprised to see Brad and Dawn walk into the room. I immediately left my desk and led them outside the building. He chatted with me for a few minutes, saying nothing important and acting as if he had done nothing unusual. Then they left the campus.

I wondered, *Is he checking up on me, or is he doing these things just to embarrass me?* It started to become obvious to me that when Brad found out I had been invited to do something, such as join the local garden club, he would find a task for me to do at the exact time of the meeting so I couldn't attend. Again, I asked myself what his motive could be. I knew if I asked him why he was doing it, he would deny it and tell me I was crazy.

When I joined a wellness center that fall, Brad accused me of going there to meet men. I assured him that was not the case—I just wanted to look nice in my clothes for him. From then on, he tried to keep me occupied by giving me busywork to do and taking me with him to equipment auctions all over the United States.

When he told me about an upcoming trip to an auction in St. Louis, Missouri, I convinced him to include a stop at Branson, Missouri, the Live Show Capital of the World. We had dinner there and saw a country music performance before heading back to our hotel room. I was discovering how nice it was to add side trips like that, especially when we visited places I had never been, such as when we went to New Orleans on a two-day business trip. We had dinner at Antoine's Restaurant in the French Quarter, where Brad ordered their famous Hurricane drink for us to sip as we walked down Bourbon Street to a jazz club. Those excursions made the drudgery of traveling with him more bearable for me.

Another fun trip we took was in October to see the foliage in Maine, where we rented a car and toured the coastline. We spotted a Fresh Lobsters sign and followed the directions down backroads to a restaurant. It was a small local place on the water and nothing fancy. When we walked in, Brad announced to the waitress that he wanted the biggest lobster they had. She told him to go over to the tank and pick out the one he wanted. When he saw how huge the lobsters were, he quickly backed down and told her, "I'll take a regular-sized lobster." Two local guys sitting at the table next to ours then spoke up and told us they were going to order another beer just so they could stay and watch Brad eat the huge lobster.

We once stayed in a house in Kennebunkport on the other side of the water from the Bush compound, and I was thrilled when I saw Barbara Bush outside with her dogs. At a local restaurant, our waitress told us Barbara and George sometimes came there to eat. "Gee," I said. "I'm sorry we missed them."

The day before our second Thanksgiving dinner, Brad flew down to Wilmington to get members of my family. Brad's family joined us the next day for the feast I had prepared, which everyone enjoyed. My family stayed with us for a few more days, so we went shopping on Black Friday to look for Christmas gifts. I had also purchased tickets for us to go to a play on Friday night. Late Saturday afternoon, I went with Brad to fly them back home.

Again, Brad reminded me that we had to have the first Christmas party of the year. We decided to invite more people that year, so our party would be larger than it had been last year. I told Brad that Ida Mae and I would need help with the food, and he quickly agreed to hire a small catering service as well as our usual bartender. I spent a lot of time making sure the menu and decorations were perfect. The occasion also gave me a reason to shop for a new cocktail dress and shoes.

After a quiet New Year's Eve at home, we packed for our

month-long stay in Florida. However, after only two days at Key Colony Beach, Brad said, "I need to leave for a few days because of things going on at work." He didn't return until the following weekend. Since I hadn't had much fun being there by myself, I suggested we cut our stay short. It made Brad happy not to be tied down in one place.

Chapter 25

YEAR FOUR

RIVERWOOD ESTATE

After the holidays, time flew by for me because we were always traveling, giving a social affair, or attending a social affair. Martin's friends were at the age for marriage, so we went to many formal weddings. The same was true about funerals due to the old age of Brad's parents and aunts and uncles.

Our weekends were filled with all kinds of fun activities. I especially enjoyed the beautiful spring weekend when Brad flew my mother and me to Michigan to attend Uncle Calvin and Aunt Sally's fiftieth wedding anniversary party. When we arrived, Brad excused himself by telling the family he had been flying with precious cargo on board and needed to rest for a while. My cousins gave their parents a big celebratory event at a local country club. It was a family affair that we thoroughly enjoyed, and I got to see relatives I hadn't seen in many years.

That summer, we took a weekend trip to the Tides Inn, where Brad showed more of his belief that rules applied to other people but not him. There were signs posted everywhere that said, "Do not walk on the grass," but he ignored them and took off walking across a beautifully manicured lawn. I was humiliated to see other guests watching him, but when I pointed the signs out to him, he not only stayed on the grass but also got mad at me because I wanted to obey the signs. I had to give in and follow him onto the lawn because I didn't want to be left behind, but I was so embarrassed that I kept my head down and wished the earth would open up and swallow me.

Although I got to visit many interesting places when I traveled with Brad, most of the time, I didn't get to see much of the area because he was always in a frenzy to get back to his business.

"I do more in a week than most people do in a month," he bragged.

It's because you're so fidgety, I thought. He was even like that with friends. A couple we knew invited us to spend the night on their boat docked at Gwynn's Island. The next morning, Brad was in such a hurry to leave that we left before anyone else was up, so we didn't even thank them for inviting us or say goodbye.

Every September, we attended a weekend at the Wintergreen resort sponsored by one of Brad's suppliers for their most valued customers. While I was unpacking, Brad left the room to go see if anyone he knew had arrived. When he returned, he had a big wrapped gift box for me. Inside was a tennis outfit, including matching tennis shoes and an expensive tennis racket.

"What is this all about?" I asked.

"I signed you up to play in the tennis tournament."

"Oh my God, Brad, why would you do that? You know I don't play tennis." In previous years, Brad had always signed himself up to play in the tournament, in which guests played against each other, but I never had because I didn't know how to play. I had never even been on a tennis court until I moved to Riverwood. Even then, I had only practiced hitting the ball back and forth without learning the rules or keeping score.

"Don't worry. You'll do fine," he said. "Let's get out of here and find the bar. That's where everyone will meet and greet."

The tennis tournament started the next morning. Although the people on my team greeted me with enthusiasm, by the end of the first set, they weren't happy with me, and I was sure they thought I was nuts for playing. I apologized for not knowing how to play and put the blame on Brad for signing me up without my consent. I was so embarrassed that I excused myself from playing and returned to our room.

Going to church on Sunday mornings changed too. Brad sat in the car with the engine running and talked on the phone while I secured the house. When I got into the car, he always asked, "What took you so long? Why were you so slow?" He sometimes rolled the windows down to vent his irritation by intentionally letting the wind blow my just-styled hair. But by the time we arrived at the church and went inside, he always reached to hold my hand.

Dawn sometimes went with us to church. She was still too young to understand what was going on during the service, so I would give her paper to draw on to help her pass the time. One Sunday, on the way home, she started whining about a stomachache. Brad got gruff with her and called her a sissy baby, which made her cry. I was shocked at how mean he was to Dawn, his precious little granddaughter, and I held her in my arms all the way home. When I told Laura that I didn't like Brad's mean behavior toward Dawn, she didn't comment and didn't even act surprised.

That evening after dinner, I became nauseated and started throwing up. I spent the entire night on the bathroom floor, but thankfully, I felt better the next morning. Laura called and said she and Dawn had been sick all night too. Brad didn't catch whatever we had. Laura said he never got sick and didn't seem to understand or sympathize when other people did.

The next day, I still felt sick, so I told Brad I couldn't go with him to an auction we had planned to attend that evening. He berated me for saying I was too sick to go, so I went to the guesthouse to get away from him. Laura happened to be passing by and followed me in to see how I was feeling. When I told her Brad had cursed at me, she replied, "I know. Dad goes to church, but he doesn't live by a word of it." That pretty much confirmed in my mind that I wasn't the one making our marriage difficult.

Since Brad was now either extremely loving or incredibly

mean, I finally decided he must have a split personality. I never knew if he was going to be respectful or mean to me or anyone he encountered. I was mortified by his rude behavior to other people and made excuses to them. He even had a meltdown when he didn't like the way an alterations lady hemmed a pair of pants for him. She never forgot his rudeness and continued to remind me about it every time I took new clothes to her for alterations.

One time, at a restaurant, Brad started harassing our waitress and actually got up from the table and followed her into the kitchen. She ignored him, so he finally returned to our table and continued eating his dinner. On the other hand, when we had drinks at the Jefferson Hotel, he kept a pleasant conversation going with one particular waitress the whole time we were there. He was so overly friendly toward her that she started flirting with him right in front of me. He didn't seem to be aware or care that it made me feel uncomfortable.

The next time I saw Brad's mother, Vivian, I told her about his bad behavior and how bewildered I was by how much he had changed since we got married.

"Brad is unstable," she said. "Even as a child, he had times when he sort of went crazy. He was always getting into trouble at school, so his teachers were constantly calling me about some nonsense he had gotten himself into. When he was growing up, it seemed that everyone who knew my son was eager to tell me a negative story about him."

"The same thing is true with me," I replied.

She went on to say, "He didn't date much either. I think he married Nancy because she was the only one who stuck with him. He always wanted a pretty woman who looked like a model and wore beautiful clothes. That's what you are, Christina—a lovely woman with so many beautiful clothes that you never wear the same thing twice."

She also told me that Nancy had said he did some things that weren't fit for a mother's ears to hear.

I felt better after talking to Vivian. I liked her, even though

Brad didn't. She was an artist, but he hated her work and refused to have any of her paintings at Riverwood. Even so, she always invited us to her art shows. We went once, and Brad couldn't leave fast enough. Sometimes when we had plans to go to a play or concert, Brad would have a crazy spell, as Vivian called it, and disappear. I often invited Vivian to go with me instead and always had a lovely time.

Chapter 26

YEAR FOUR
RIVERWOOD ESTATE

Brad and I noticed that Laura and Dawn often left home early in the morning and were gone until almost dark. Brad assumed she was going to her mother's house to spend the day while Sam slept. Nancy had not returned to Laura's house after Brad forbid her from coming back on the property. During their separation, Brad had cut down a few trees to expand his runway. When Nancy saw what he had done, she'd told Laura and Martin that he had damaged the property, so their inheritance was worth less money. Brad had had a tree expert talk to Laura and Martin to tell them that no damage had been done because the trees could reproduce themselves. From then on, Brad would not let Nancy come back because he felt she was spying on him and causing unrest between him and his children.

Brad also suspected Nancy was undermining him in the community as well. He had recently applied to join a prestigious club in Charlottesville that required an applicant to have six sponsors from the club's seven hundred members in order to be considered by the membership committee. He told me that although he had met with potential sponsors, he wasn't accepted for membership because they didn't like his behavior when he was married to Nancy. That news came as a shock to me and made me question what Brad had previously told me about his marriage. According to him, his divorce from Nancy had been amicable, but I was beginning to think it might have been an ugly and public divorce. When we'd married, he already had been a member of the two select clubs we now belonged to, so his suspicions about Nancy were probably right, I thought.

When Nutmeg needed to go to the vet for his checkup that fall, I called Dawn and asked if she would like to go with me. She said yes and told me Nutmeg was at her house. As I drove the short distance to their house, I saw immediately that Nancy's car was parked in front. Laura ran out with Nutmeg and hurriedly pushed him into my car. I could tell she was uneasy. Dawn decided not to go to the vet with me because she wanted to visit with her grandmother. As I was leaving, I met Brad coming down the driveway. He could easily see Nancy's car, and he was furious. That led to his giving Laura an ultimatum to either tell Nancy to never come onto the property again or move off the property herself. Laura didn't want to tell her mother to stay away, so she and Brad were on the outs after that.

The straw that broke the camel's back happened a few weeks later, when Ida Mae told Brad she had seen Sam filling up their Jeep with gas from Brad's farm equipment gas tank. That provoked Brad even further. A few days later, Laura came over to visit with me. We were sitting at the kitchen table, having coffee, when Brad came charging through the door. He glowered at Laura and said, "I thought I made myself perfectly clear when I told you I didn't want your mother back on this property. You've ignored me, so go start packing to move."

I quickly left the room, but I could still hear their loud voices and profane words as they argued. Laura left without speaking to me. I knew she must have been upset. I returned to the kitchen and pressed both hands to Brad's chest. "I love having Dawn so close. Please don't make them move." He waved me off without a word, ignoring my plea. I thought, *Why is he doing this? I just can't see his point.*

After that, Brad stopped giving Laura the monthly allowance

she had been getting from the business. She had never had to pay rent or utilities because their house was part of the Riverwood Estate. With no income, Laura and her family had no choice but to move in with her mother.

Not long after the day I took Nutmeg to the vet, Nutmeg was hit by a car and killed on the busy highway in front of Riverwood. I had reminded Brad many times of the likelihood of that happening because of the way Nutmeg would pick up a scent and follow it for miles. Brad's response was that he used to have two other basset hounds that did the same thing, and nothing had ever happened to them. I pointed out that the area had grown up since then and had more traffic now.

Brad started researching dog breeds to replace Nutmeg. I wanted a small dog I could keep inside and easily bathe. A country dog that stayed outside was hard to keep groomed. Brad would not hear of getting a little dog. He said they were for sissies, so he brought home an Old English sheepdog puppy that was friendly and cute. We named him Gatsby. He and our cat quickly became friends, and they stayed together most of the time. On cold nights, when I brought them inside, they slept together. Since Brad never brushed Gatsby, his coat often got so matted that it had to be sheared. For Brad's birthday that year, an employee called to ask me what would be a good gift for him, and I suggested a gift certificate to have Gatsby groomed. When Brad was contacted by the grooming company to set up an appointment, he told them to keep their hands off his dog. His response dumbfounded me.

Chapter 27

YEAR FOUR
RIVERWOOD ESTATE

As time went on, I learned more and more about Brad's erratic behavior and how he tried to keep people off balance and dependent on him so he could have control of them, including me. I became aware that he lied all the time about everything, even when he didn't need to and when there was no point. Brad's life was constructed on lies and half-truths. I was also discovering the unethical way Brad ran his business. He would fire people at the drop of a hat and then rehire them just to keep them off balance. He deliberately chose to surround himself with dishonest employees and professionals, such as his attorney, Michael Kelton, whom he apparently controlled through blackmail of some sort.

After Brad's office manager quit, he decided the company was getting so large that he needed to add a CPA to his staff. When he placed the help-wanted ad, one of the applicants was Regan Miller, a certified CPA who had done prison time for embezzling money from his previous company. Brad hired him and was soon visited by Regan's parole officer, who would be checking in with him every month. If Brad gave the officer a negative report, Regan could go back to prison, so Brad had control over him.

When state inspectors went to job sites, Brad instructed his employees to keep them occupied as much as possible so they wouldn't see any violations. He even told his vehicle safety inspector to look the other way when certain repairs were needed. Since Brad flew an airplane, he could go anywhere he wanted on weekdays. His employees were instructed to cover for him, so if I called for him during the day, I was never sure whether or not they were telling me the truth about where he was. I sometimes went with Brad to meetings where company representatives met to bid on jobs. I once overheard him mention price fixing and bid rigging to Martin, and I could tell from the way they were talking that those kinds of activities were illegal. I assumed he was watching out for other companies that might be doing it so he wouldn't lose jobs to them.

Chapter 28

One evening during the summer of our fourth year of marriage, I was in the kitchen preparing dinner, when I heard the roar of the Gulfstream jet engines coming over the James River. Then I heard the loudest thud imaginable, and the house shook. When I frantically looked out the kitchen window, I could see the plane sliding on its belly down the grassy part of the runway that ran by the house. I ran to the front door and saw the plane still sliding, coming up onto the concrete part of the runway with sparks flying. I started running toward the tilted plane but quickly realized I was too far away and probably couldn't get the aircraft door open anyway, so I ran back into the house to call 911. The dispatcher asked if a fire truck were needed, but there was no sign of fire, so I said no. While I was still on the phone, I ran back outside and saw Brad walking up the road leading to the main house. I ran to meet him, and he said he was okay and didn't need medical assistance. I then told the dispatcher, "Everything is fine," and I ended the call.

As usual, Brad immediately called Martin, who came home from work right away. They were sitting on the porch drinking beer when an FAA representative showed up unexpectedly to get details about the plane crash. After the representative left, Brad told me his beer drinking was in the report. With his eyes narrowed and his fists clenched, he reprimanded me harshly for calling 911, which had caused the FAA to be notified to investigate the crash. The official reason for the accident was that the landing gear had failed and collapsed, or maybe Brad had just forgotten to put down the landing gear. No one will know the answer to that except Brad.

I had become a seasoned flier by then. When Graham or Martin wasn't with us, I sat in the copilot's seat. I liked being able to hear what was going on between Brad and the tower and look out for nearby aircraft. I kept a close eye on the gauges and asked him questions if a reading changed, particularly when the fuel gauge started getting low. Brad began relying on me to look up airport call letters in the flight manual, which made me feel important. I paid close attention to the weather radar to see if we needed to divert around any thunderstorms in the area. There were times when we had to land and wait for bad weather to pass. Being surrounded by clouds and flying blind made me glad when we could see blue sky again and when our ride was less bumpy. Just prior to landing, I always reminded Brad to double-check everything that needed to be done for a safe landing, especially making sure the landing gear was down and locked in position. I hadn't forgotten about his accident.

About a month after Brad's plane crash, we were on the side porch, enjoying our after-dinner drinks, when out of the blue, he said the premiums on the life insurance policy he'd taken out for me were so high that it was a hardship on the business to keep paying them. I didn't want to hurt the company or appear greedy, so I agreed for him to cancel the policy. In exchange, he told me he was going to put something extra for me in his will. He carried his handwritten will in his back pocket and changed it almost daily as another way of controlling people. He could take people out of the will as easily as he could put them in.

Later that spring, I went to visit my mother in Wilmington for a week. When I was ready to go home and went to the airport to meet Brad, I was surprised to see a woman in the Baron's pilot seat. She told me she was friends with Brad, and since she was working on getting her license to fly a multiengine airplane, he had offered to let her make that trip to get in more hours. She had a male instructor copilot with her, so I sat in the backseat instead of up front, as I usually did. On the trip home, I told her I appreciated her coming to get me and wished there had been time to show her the area. When she didn't respond, I thought she hadn't heard me because of the engine noise, so I repeated more loudly that I would have liked to show her around my hometown. I noticed her hands tighten around the steering wheel, and she turned her head away as if she didn't want to say anything. I was surprised at her reaction, but finally, she turned back toward me and said she was familiar with the area because she had been there with Brad when he wanted to go for a swim in the ocean.

I was shocked and couldn't believe what I had just heard. I remained quiet the rest of the way home. Brad had never mentioned anything about that to me. When I got home, I let him know how unhappy I was about his trip to the beach and how embarrassing it had been for both the pilot and me when I found out about it. As I entered my dressing room to unpack my suitcase, I noticed an article of my clothing out of place. I immediately turned to Brad and asked, "Why is my dress lying on this chair?"

"Oh, I was just showing someone your beautiful clothes," he answered casually.

I was too angry about his deceitfulness to even ask who the person was, but I thought it was probably the same female pilot who'd gone swimming with him in Wilmington. I wondered what else was going on that I hadn't yet discovered about Brad's relationship with the young woman. How did he know her so well that he trusted her with his expensive company airplane?

That year, when we went to Hilton Head to see the tennis tournaments, Brad's office called to tell us our housekeeper, Ida Mae, had found the house flooded when she went to work that morning. A pipe that had just been repaired in an upstairs bathroom had sprung a major leak. Since the bathroom was on the third floor, water had seeped down through the floor to the main living area and soaked the furniture and rugs. Water had even run out of the entrance chandelier like a faucet.

When the plumber had been there for the repair in the upstairs bathroom, I had asked him to show me where the cutoff valve for the whole house was located. I'd then showed it to Ida Mae just so she would know, but she apparently hadn't understood or maybe had just forgotten, because she tried to mop up the water instead of cutting it off. When she eventually realized that water was still coming in, she called Brad's office, and they sent someone out to cut the water off. By that time, the water had also seeped down through the main floor into the basement area, so another big oriental rug there got wet, as well as all the papers in the filing cabinet and office.

A significant amount of plaster work was needed to repair all the damage. The workmen erected scaffolding everywhere in the house so that it was difficult to walk from one area of the house to another. When they started sanding, the air was thick with plaster dust that settled all over everything. I asked Brad if we could stay in a motel for a few days during the worst of it, but he refused. I stood it as long as I could, but I eventually checked into a motel by myself for two nights, which infuriated him. That incident again showed me his controlling ways and reinforced that he wasn't thoughtful about my being inconvenienced.

While the repair work was being done, I thought of the endless repairs my house in Williamsburg would have needed if I had kept it. I said to Brad, "I'm glad I sold my house."

He quickly responded, "Too bad you sold it—you might have to move back there." I assumed he said that because of all the things I was doing that didn't suit him, and he was trying to make me fearful—after all, his list was growing longer.

Chapter 29

What Brad had envisioned and planned for was finally happening: Martin was following in his footsteps and would someday soon take over the business. Since Martin was young and impressionable, he conformed to Brad's business practices without argument as to whether they were legal or not. Brad had made sure he learned to fly the company aircraft, even though he had difficulty passing the pilot license test. Brad even sent him away to a flight school in Florida to make sure he passed the test. Martin was used to a privileged lifestyle.

Martin had recently gotten angry with Brad and walked off the job. After he stayed home and thought for a while, he called Brad with apologies and asked for his job back. According to Brad, Martin said, "You own my house, my car, and my job. I need to come back to work for you."

"Since Martin has returned to work," Brad told me, "he has been an outstanding employee." The thought crossed my mind that with Martin so dependent on him, Brad had the control he wanted over him.

Martin was into heavy partying, which Brad encouraged and thought was funny. When Martin brought friends to Riverwood, Brad always made their drinks extra strong and joked with them about women. Martin often flew his friends to football games and other events and then drank so much that the next day, he would have to leave the aircraft and take a commercial flight back home. Then Brad would have to fly him back in one of the other planes so Martin could fly the party plane home. When I mentioned to Brad how extravagant Martin was, his comeback to me was that Martin was a hard worker and deserved to make a good salary.

"But you aren't teaching him to be a responsible person," I said. Then Brad would accuse me of begrudging his children because I didn't like them, but I was only trying to be helpful. To justify Martin's spending, Brad would remind me that the UPS truck came every day to bring things I had purchased on his credit card, forgetting that he demanded I always look like a model and wear fabulous outfits.

Martin and his girlfriend, Addison, had an off-and-on relationship. It appeared he wasn't ready to settle down because he was enjoying playing around too much. It seemed no matter what he did, she'd take him back, even when he showed up on her doorstep drunk after partying all night with another woman. Brad and Martin laughed about that, calling Addison the Doormat.

Brad often waited until the last minute to tell me he and Martin were going hunting—or doing anything else, for that matter. He would rush into the house and gather some clothes, and when I asked him what he was doing, he'd say he hadn't told me sooner because I would have gotten upset that he was doing something with Martin since I didn't like his children. I didn't care if he went somewhere with Martin, but it would have been courteous of him to tell me he was going out of town.

I detected a clue of Brad's obsession with Martin when we saw a pair of silver-plated candelabras for three candles in an antique store. Even though Christmas was still months away, Brad thought they would be a good Christmas present for Martin. I couldn't help but think, *What young man would want silver candlesticks for a Christmas present?*

The candelabras I was presently using on the dining room table at Riverwood were enormous and ornate, almost too large to use during dinner parties. I decided I might like the ones Brad had just bought better. When we got home, I saw how perfect the smaller candlesticks looked on our dining room table and asked him, "Can we keep these and get something else for Martin?"

Brad replied, "I bought those candlesticks for Martin," and he snatched them and took off walking down to Martin's house. He gave me the clear message that Martin was more important than my feelings.

Chapter 30

After several years of dating Addison, Martin finally decided to marry her. His reason, he said, was that he'd dated other girls but always ended up back with her. I could never see what Addison wanted with Martin. He couldn't even spell her name correctly. He was good looking and made lots of money, but he was a spendthrift. Addison's father said that if she managed the family finances after they were married, everything would be okay.

They began to plan possibly the largest wedding ever seen in the area. Addison's father was well off, so he was ready for the big expense.

When Martin got engaged, I reminded Brad about our prenuptial contract and asked about the risk Martin had when he got married. Brad replied, "We have that covered." He went on to explain that he had three sets of company stock certificates hidden away. One had both his and Martin's names on it, one had only Martin's name on it, and the other had only Brad's name on it. That way, if he got sued, he would show the certificate with Martin's name to prove he didn't own the company, and vice versa if Martin got sued. Having the fake documents gave each of them protection in case of a divorce too.

As part of their wedding preparations, Addison and Martin

purchased a house together near the main office in Charlottesville, but they couldn't move in before the wedding because that would upset her parents. For the same reason, they had never let her parents know about her sleepovers with him over the past years or about her drinking and smoking.

Martin moved into the house first and started a big renovation. When Brad and I were over there one night, Martin and Addison were frustrated because they felt the previous owners were being uncooperative about something they were supposed to repair. Brad found a set of keys the old owners had left and threw them as far as he could into the woods, saying they would never find those keys. Addison said, "I'm glad Brad is on our side and not against us."

Martin wanted to have the rehearsal dinner at Ruth Chris Steak House. He invited all his groomsmen and insisted they bring dates, which wasn't customary. He offered unlimited bar drinks for everyone. Since Martin was used to getting whatever he wanted, that was what Brad gave him.

Addison and her parents settled on the historic Rosemont Manor for the wedding venue. It was a memorable outdoor wedding. The food was delicious, and the live band played on and on. After the cake cutting, the bride and groom departed by a horse-drawn carriage. The next day, they left for a weeklong honeymoon in St. Thomas. Martin called Brad every day to tell him how bored he was.

As soon as they returned from their honeymoon, Martin told us he wanted to start having babies right away. "Oh no, Martin," Addison said in protest. "I want to postpone pregnancy for at least a year. By that time, I'll be ready to quit my teaching job." Her willingness to start a family in a year seemed to stop Martin's pushing her to get pregnant immediately.

When Martin went back to work running the main business office, Brad felt he was doing an excellent job, so he turned all of his attention to the satellite offices and bidding for new jobs. Brad's desire was for Martin and his family to have the best of everything, and because he had willed me one-third of the business, he wanted to make sure I could do nothing to upset the business if something happened to him. Brad's actions toward me made that a known fact. I became their enemy. I thought Brad and Martin must have discussed the matter often. I felt as if Brad were married to Martin instead of me. Martin was always put first and could do no wrong. I thought I would scream if I heard "You don't like my children" or "You begrudge my children" one more time.

Chapter 31

YEAR FIVE

RIVERWOOD ESTATE

Paula Simon, a member of our church congregation, was an heir to her family-owned winery just outside of Charlottesville. Every time we attended a church social, her longtime friend George approached Brad about buying the winery. He told Brad, "With Paula's family getting older, there will soon be no one left to run the winery, so the family is ready to sell."

Initially, the offer didn't seem to interest Brad, but over time, as George kept talking to him on Paula's behalf, he finally agreed to go look at the property. When Martin found out about the possibility of owning a winery, he behaved like a spoiled child, prancing around with excitement and encouraging Brad to buy it. "Dad, let's get this. I can see the name Hightower Winery on the wine bottle now."

Brad met with Paula to learn about the operational aspects of the winery. With Martin's strong encouragement, he was finally convinced to make an offer to buy it. The winery had been a family-owned business for several generations, so as the new owner, Brad created quite a bit of interest.

When the negotiations started, Paula was her family's spokesperson. During that time, whenever we had a party at Riverwood, Paula continued to be at the top of Brad's guest list, and she would usually bring George as her date. At Brad's insistence, we met them for drinks a few times too. I could tell meeting us wasn't something George really wanted to do. Although he and Brad had gone to the same school as children, they were not friends.

I considered Paula to be a friend, though not a close one. She invited us to her parties and always sat behind us at church services. She even knelt next to me to take communion. When Paula and her sister invited me to go to a garden home show with them, I readily accepted. At the show, they asked me so many questions about Brad that I became hoarse from answering them. They wanted to know everything about him and what it was like to be married to him.

While Brad was negotiating to buy the winery, I often accompanied him when he went there to go over the books. That gave me the opportunity to meet the office manager, Jennifer, and we struck up a friendship. The winery was located about twenty miles from Riverwood and was near our church, so much of our social life was already in that area.

Brad's lawyer recommended that since Brad and I owned no assets together, we should acquire joint property, so we looked at houses to buy near the winery because there would be times when traveling back and forth from the winery wouldn't be practical. Having a house there would also make us part of the community.

Brad told me he occasionally met with Paula for business lunches. Then his behavior toward me started to change. I noticed that if I got up in the morning before he left the house, he would start a fight about something and would have me running around like a mother getting a young child off to school. One morning, he couldn't find an important paper and accused me of hiding it from him, even though I was helping him look for it. I thought his impatience with me might be because of the pressure he was under to finalize the purchase of the winery, so I phoned Paula and asked if she could speed up the negotiations so Brad would have a closing date.

Brad's verbal abuse continued. When he was angry with me, he'd say, "You're nothing. You came from nothing. Go back to nothing," and "It cost me a million dollars to marry you." Brad said my parents didn't love me because they had given me away. I had once told him I used to spend nights with my sick great-aunt Elva. She had no children, so after her husband died when I was in the fifth grade, she and my parents decided I would spend the night with her every night after having dinner at home with my family. She lived only two blocks away, so I could walk or ride my bike to her house. The next morning, after breakfast, I would go back home and then go to school with my sister. I did that every day until I left to go to college in New York City. I had just graduated when she died, and I was the only beneficiary of her estate. I never felt I had been given away by my parents, but Brad would throw it in my face when he was angry with me.

One hot day, during the negotiations, Brad decided to take a few of his employees on a day trip to Ocracoke Island, and he wanted me to go too. I agreed but told him I felt a bit ill and might not be able to do everything they did. That was okay with him at that time.

When we got to the island, he rented bikes so everyone could ride to the beach, which was a good distance away. We had flown there, so we had no car and had already walked from the plane to the bike rental place. The day was so scorching hot that I felt as if I were going to pass out from the heat. As we rode our bikes to the beach, I kept falling farther and farther behind. My bike was in such bad shape that it was difficult to pedal. I finally stopped and went into an air-conditioned store where I could cool off. When Brad discovered I was missing, he returned to find me and said, "You have embarrassed me in front of my employees and ruined our trip." In no way was he sensible or understanding about my being overheated and sick.

Shortly after Brad was so critical of me, the chain on Martin's bike came off and caused him to fall and scrape his knee and leg so badly that we had to go back home immediately so a doctor could pick the gravel out of his wounds. Brad said nothing about our trip being cut short because of Martin's bike accident.

Brad also seemed to get enjoyment out of frightening me. We kept our boat at a marina in Wrightsville Beach, North Carolina, where we often spent weekends and where his children and their families joined us for two weeks every summer. He seemed to take delight in driving the boat at top speed just to scare me. One time, Dawn was in the boat with us, and Brad went so fast that I was fearful the child would go flying out of the boat. I held on to her for dear life and pleaded with Brad to slow down. Another time when he was going full speed ahead, he aimed the boat straight for pilings and forced me to take the steering wheel. I panicked, begging him over and over to take the wheel back. He did the same thing to me one time in the Cherokee plane, making me take the controls when I didn't have a clue how to keep the plane level.

As time went on that year, when we traveled somewhere special, such as the Tides Inn, Nantucket, the Greenbrier, or Martha's Vineyard, Brad would get mad at me for no real reason and then blame me for spoiling the trip. At Nantucket, we were parked looking out over the moonlit water, when he started fussing at me about something I had done or said that he didn't like. I was so upset that I started crying and decided I was going to leave him when I got back home. However, before we left the island, he turned on his charm and bought me a Nantucket basket necklace to get back in my good graces. I didn't want to go through the discomfiture of another failed marriage, so I prayed our marriage would work out. When his cruelty kept occurring, I eventually figured out that Brad would back off when he pushed me to tears but not before.

One day I was in a bookstore and happened to see a book entitled *Verbal Abuse*, which sparked my interest. After reading only a few pages, I knew that was what I was experiencing, because Brad's words and actions were hurting me over and over again. I had never heard of verbal abuse or experienced anything like his controlling ways before, so I didn't recognize what was happening to me. From reading the book, I learned that verbal abuse could turn into physical abuse, so I continued doing everything I could to find out how to counter his bullying behavior.

Our Thanksgiving gathering that year again included family members I didn't get to see often. Aunt Sally couldn't wait to bring me up to date on what my six cousins were doing. We all enjoyed the Thanksgiving feast I'd prepared, and as usual, we all ate too much. Afterward, everyone headed for the TV to watch the football game while Mother helped me put the leftover food away and start the dishwasher. During halftime, Addison and Martin stood up and made a big announcement: "We're expecting a baby boy in June." Everyone congratulated them and gave them big hugs.

Our annual Christmas party had grown into a large catered affair attended by judges and other dignitaries as well as close friends and acquaintances. I spent a lot of time making sure the decorations and food selections were perfect, and I picked out a ravishing new cocktail dress. During the party, a few guests who were members of our church approached me and asked if I would be willing to have a fund-raiser at Riverwood to benefit the church.

"Christina, you have done such a marvelous job of decorating this historical house," said one member. "I'm sure we could sell many tickets for a tour of your home."

"I'll give this some thought and get back with you," I said.

When I spoke with Brad about opening our home to strangers, he initially refused to even think about it. I won the disagreement when members started thanking him for considering an open house to raise money for the church. I put together an advertising brochure that gave a detailed room-by-room description of the inside of the house to make people want to buy a tour ticket.

Chapter 32

JANUARY TO OCTOBER, YEAR SIX
RIVERWOOD ESTATE

At last, the negotiations with Paula's family ended. The winery deal was closed, and Brad took ownership on the first day of January. Building an airplane runway on the property so Brad's planes could come in and out made him the talk of the town. He went to the winery almost every day but stayed overnight only occasionally.

In early April, Laura called our house for the first time since Brad had made her move away from Riverwood. That evening, when I told him about her call, he said she had also called the office and wanted to meet with him the next day. It was easy to figure out why she was calling: she and her family were desperate. Not long ago, they had moved from Nancy's house to a tiny two-bedroom house, and by then, their car had probably fallen apart too. It was the first time she and Sam had ever had to pay rent, utility bills, and all the other bills life required.

Sure enough, when Brad saw Laura the next day, she asked for a job, so he put her to work at the winery. He had found out that Jennifer, who had been the winery's office manager for thirty years, wouldn't falsify reports and the like, as Evelyn did for him at the main office. He even told her that if she went to jail, he would visit her. Despite Jennifer knowing all the ins and outs of how the winery operated, Brad fired her and told her to go home and work in her flower garden. Then he made Laura the new office manager. In no time, she and her family were moving into a large house, she was driving a new company SUV, and Dawn was attending a private school. Life was good again, except Brad once more had control over her just as he did with Martin. Brad was the head of their households.

Brad began spending more and more time away from home. His reason, he said, was that he was going places and doing things with Martin and Laura. I was getting tired of being left alone and sick of hearing "You don't like my children" if I expressed any frustration. One night in May, when Brad was gone all night, I had a little too much wine to drink. I was mad and upset about his behavior toward me, so I wrote him a note that said, "Since you are spending so much time with Martin and Laura, you should have sex with them and leave me alone."

Brad came home early the next morning before I got up, found the note, and went berserk. He told me he was leaving me because the note was so repulsive. He then started spending even more nights at the winery and claimed we were separated. But sometimes he would stay at Riverwood and act as if nothing were wrong in our marriage, and then he would go back to the winery. Sometimes he even asked me to come spend nights with him there, which I did several times. He had turned one of the office cubicles into a bedroom and installed a shower. I was never comfortable staying there because of my fear of someone breaking into the office. Brad kept a loaded gun by the bed just in case.

I confided in Paula about Brad's strange behavior and suggested the two of us go out to dinner sometime. Her response was that I should take care of myself at a time like that. She couldn't get rid of me fast enough.

I visited Addison to take her a baby gift and mentioned how secretive Brad was about what he was doing and what was going on in the business. Although she praised Martin for telling her everything, she refused to help me because she didn't want to get involved. She gave me the impression she didn't want to upset her gravy train by befriending me, the enemy.

When I happened to notice that the personal money he had been giving me for helping with the business entertaining and running the house was no longer being put into my account, I asked Brad about it. He couldn't come up with a good answer and mostly ignored my inquiry. I thought to myself that meant all the promises he had made to me concerning my marriage security had been broken. In late May, he came home and threw a handful of papers onto the entrance hall sideboard.

"Here," he said with a sneer. "This should make you feel better." I looked at the papers, and they said that in the event of Brad's death, Martin would get everything, including the cash on hand. I was furious.

"What do you mean? My interpretation of these papers is that Martin will get everything, right down to the change in your pocket."

"They don't say that!" Brad yelled.

The argument escalated, as did my anger and frustration at his insanity. My heart was pounding in my chest, and I was suddenly trembling from being so angry. I turned and ran upstairs to my dressing room. I threw myself onto my chaise lounge and tried to take deep breaths to calm myself down. Brad came stomping upstairs after me, still screaming that the papers didn't say that. He loomed over me with his teeth clenched and his hands in fists. He was so threatening that I picked up the phone receiver and said, "I'm going to call 911 if you don't leave me alone." He lunged for the receiver, squeezing my hand as hard as he could and twisting it. I felt my wrist and fingers crack with excruciating pain and screamed. He yanked the receiver away and started beating me on the back of my head with it. I instinctively tried to cover my head with my hands, which left the back of my neck exposed to his repeated blows. Even though my eyes were tightly shut, I could see bright lights flashing every time he hit me. I was in shock, screaming and writhing, trying to get away from him.

I was inexplicitly caught in an unbelievable act of violence that I thought would never end.

When he finally threw down the receiver and stormed out of the room, I was curled up so tightly that I could barely breathe. I began to gasp loudly, my chest heaving with the effort of getting air back into my lungs. My head was spinning and throbbing with agonizing pain. Then I was suddenly seized with fear that he had done irreparable damage to my body. I carefully sat up and sighed with relief that I could still wiggle my fingers and toes.

I heard Brad yell from downstairs once again that I didn't know what I was talking about. Then he slammed the front door, and I heard the car start up. I cautiously stood up, looked out the window, and saw the taillights of his car going down the driveway. As my terror subsided, it was replaced by a raging fury I had never experienced before. I made my way downstairs on wobbly legs and then picked up the first thing I saw—a vase of roses—and threw it across the room. The crystal vase exploded with a satisfying crash, and only my shaky legs kept me from stomping the roses into the rug.

Gradually, my anger subsided to a determination to leave Riverwood by any means possible. I searched through the telephone book for an organization that helped battered women. I couldn't find any such agency, and the places I did call were closed. I resolved to try again in the morning and began to slowly clean up the big mess I had made. I didn't want Ida Mae to find it the next morning or Brad to find it if he happened to come back home. By the time I finished, it was late, so I collapsed into bed, exhausted and still in shock about what had just happened to me. I slept little because of my pain. *Will daylight ever come?* I wondered.

I went to see my doctor early the next morning, and he referred me to an orthopedic specialist. As it turned out, I had nerve damage in my neck and hand that required physical therapy. I wasn't able to completely close my hand, and the therapist told me she was worried about it because my injury was so severe. My pain was excruciating. I was too embarrassed to tell anyone the truth about my injuries, even the doctors. With so much damage and pain, I spent most of the day in bed, sleeping off pain medication, and was in no position to do anything about leaving Brad. I had no family in the area, and if I stayed at Riverwood, Ida Mae could do things for me while I recovered. I now believed Brad would kill anybody he thought might take something away from Martin.

Brad returned home that afternoon before Ida Mae had left for the day. I didn't hear his car drive up because I was sleeping. I woke up when he opened the bedroom door. He was carrying a tray of food for my dinner and had a sheepish look on his face, as if he weren't sure what my reaction was going to be. I assumed Ida Mae had filled him in on the results of my doctor's appointment that morning and told him I was in bed upstairs and needed to take pain medication.

After placing the tray where I could reach it, Brad sat down on the side of the bed and asked how I was feeling. Then he told me he was planning to take me to my scheduled MRI at five o'clock the next morning and then to my PT appointment in the afternoon. I was so shocked by his concern for me and so groggy that I was only able to listen without any comment to what he was saying.

He did what he said he would do and was attentive in the following evenings. By Sunday, I had improved enough that we could go to church. I had to ask Brad to drive slowly on the rough country roads because the bumps caused me to have neck pain, and he complied. He treated me with compassion and respect, and I never felt threatened by him again. He even ordered several pairs of cute shoes for me. In response to that honeymoon period, there were times when I felt a renewal of love for him. *After all*, I kept reminding myself, *the relationship has its good points. It's not all bad, and I don't want another divorce. Other women have experienced this and gotten over the pain and hurt, and I can too.* Knowing our relationship hadn't begun like that, I hoped it would change.

During one of my physical therapy treatments in June, I looked out the window at the hospital across the street, where Addison was giving birth to her and Martin's first child. Since I was now the enemy, I was not included in that family event. My emotions were torn. One side of me said it was wrong for my husband to be with his children and ex-wife, Nancy, and not include me in the joyous occasion, while the other side reminded me I was there at the rehabilitation center because of the abuse I had suffered at the hands of that husband. I became furious all over again that he thought I was so stupid I would fall for his nonsense by taking his word about the papers he had brought home without even reading them.

On my way back to Riverwood after a physical therapy treatment, I stopped by a lawyer's office and asked her if I were interpreting the wording correctly on the papers Brad had given me. After reading them, she told me I was right: Martin would get everything.

Brad's father, William, became increasingly ill and then died from cancer in July. Brad told me I shouldn't be allowed to attend his dad's funeral, but then he took me with him as if he had never made that ugly comment. Brad was acting even stranger than usual. He had always had a good supply of both alcohol and Valium on hand, so I thought he might have been overindulging because he was upset about his father.

I finally found the courage to confide in Vivian that Brad had physically hurt me. She told me her other daughter-in-law had once come to her for help after Brad's brother hit her in the eye. Vivian also told me that son had schizophrenia, and her daughter-in-law had divorced him. I later contacted her, and as we compared notes, I concluded Brad must also have mental problems.

Brad called me one day in early October and said he was having his yearly flight physical that afternoon, and he asked me to go to dinner with him afterward. When he didn't show up at the time he was supposed to pick me up, I figured he had changed his mind. Then I received a call from the doctor's office: Brad had an irregular heartbeat and was on his way to the hospital by ambulance. I was terrified and left immediately to go to the hospital. I got there before the ambulance and called Martin to tell him the bad news. When the ambulance arrived and Brad saw me, he smiled and waved as he was taken into an ER room. During his one-week hospital stay, he didn't want me to leave him. When I did leave, he would soon call me on the phone to come back. Everybody, including the reverend and me, thought he was over his crazy spell of wanting a divorce. He even wanted to have sex with me in the hospital bed. When he was discharged from the hospital, Laura picked him up and took him to Riverwood. To my surprise, they only stayed long enough to have lunch with me and then left to go to the winery.

Even though Brad claimed he was separated from me and had been living at the winery since May, he was still coming back and forth to Riverwood and living as husband and wife with me. He told me, "Let's celebrate the Thanksgiving and Christmas holidays together and then get a divorce." At any moment, he would leave and go back to the winery. Then he would see an article of clothing he liked in a magazine and order it for me, so I was constantly kept off balance.

When Brad's crazy behavior continued, I didn't know what else to do except call his lawyer, Michael Kelton, one afternoon in late October to ask him for any paperwork he might have from the prenuptial signing attempts. I was nervous about calling him because of his close relationship with Brad. I hadn't seen him since the previous year, when Brad and I had gone to see property Kelton had just bought with the intention of opening a winery. When he answered, I told him to please not hang up on me because I needed to ask him for any paperwork he had about the prenup. He replied that he had given everything he had to Brad a long time ago. He then went on to say how betrayed he'd felt when Brad bought a winery near his location, because now Brad was his competition instead of his friend. In fact, Kelton was still so angry about it that he blurted out that Brad was having an affair: "It's with Paula Simon."

I almost fainted upon hearing that my husband was having an affair. Although I was crushed, confused, and angry, I tried to keep my wits about me so I could get as much information from Kelton as possible about the affair.

For the next several days, I was in complete shock and despair. I felt like a zombie. But at last, things were starting to make some sense. I knew from seeing Paula at church that she and George had recently broken up after many years of being a couple and then gotten back together several times before having what appeared to be a final breakup. I thought, *That's why our marriage would improve and then go haywire again.*

Paula was hyper and a heavy drinker, which was probably why George never had committed to marrying her. He never had moved in with her, always keeping his home in Richmond. A behavioral pattern began to come to light: When Paula and George were together, our marriage would improve. When Paula and George broke up, things went badly for me, and Brad would go back to the winery and see Paula openly.

Chapter 33

OCTOBER TO DECEMBER, YEAR SIX
RIVERWOOD ESTATE

During those up and downs, Brad still maintained that we had separated in May, so I reminded him that our prenuptial contract had expired the previous June and was therefore no longer in effect because we had been married for more than five years. Thus, I had full rights as a wife. He kept trying to persuade me to redo our contract and told me if I did, he would come back home. I had no interest in redoing anything with Brad. I knew he would only find a way later to take away whatever we agreed on, as he had done before. I was also beginning to feel that his offer to come back home if I complied was a trick.

Sometime during that roller-coaster ride, Brad decided we should see a marriage counselor because he thought the counselor would prove he was right and I was wrong. Brad showed his crazy side in the counselor's office when I pulled something out of my billfold and my credit cards flew everywhere. Brad accused me of throwing them at him and stormed out of the office. The counselor knew that what had happened had been an accident and said to me, "Brad doesn't want to be married." We didn't go back there.

Our second try at counseling was with our pastor, Reverend Jones. Again, Brad was hoping I would be told that everything was my fault. In Reverend Jones's concluding remarks in a private session with me, he said, "What Brad liked about you while dating has become a threat to him. He doesn't know how to handle your being an independent person. His desire for complete control forces him to lose sight of why he wanted you and is why he now seeks it in others."

When all Brad's attempts to get me to renegotiate our contract failed, he made life more difficult for me. He closed our joint checking account without telling me, which caused me to write several bad checks. When I realized what he had done, I went immediately to the bank and opened a checking account in my name only so he would never be able to hurt and embarrass me that way again.

Despite Brad not having a valid FAA medical certificate because of his atrial fibrillation diagnosis, he regularly flew with Paula on out-of-town trips. As always, Brad's philosophy was that rules were for other people, not him. However, he finally got caught. The next time he came back to Riverwood, he told me he had lost his pilot's license. When he'd flown into the Charlottesville airport, an FAA agent had been waiting for him because they had received an anonymous tip that he was flying without a medical certificate. He omitted telling me the trip had been with Paula, but Jennifer had already told me. I thought, *This serves you right.* I even felt some elation about it.

That serious violation resulted in the FAA stripping Brad of all his flying credentials, which meant he not only would need to pass a flight physical before he could legally fly a plane again but also would have to take all the tests for his private pilot license and his multiengine jet and instrument ratings. He easily got his medical certificate back because he learned how to take his pulse—if his heartbeat were out of rhythm, he would not go for his flight physical. Only Brad could have deceived the FAA. After taking and passing the required tests, he was able to fly legally again.

Christmas came soon after Brad got his license back, and he spent it with me at Riverwood. On Christmas morning, he got the notion to call one of his relatives who lived in Kilmarnock, a small town about thirty minutes away by plane, and ask him to pick us up at the local airport. I had a turkey in the oven, so I just turned the oven off and walked out with Brad. When we arrived at the airport, a family member met us at the airport and drove us to the house, which was full of people who had been invited to Christmas dinner. The table was beautifully set, and we were clearly intruding, but Brad was oblivious. Nothing ever seemed to embarrass him, so I was glad when he eventually asked for a ride back to the airport so we could go back to Riverwood.

Brad never stopped telling me he would return home if I would do another contract. By then, I didn't trust him at all, so I ignored his requests. That led to more punishment from him. He said he had always known I would leave him one day, because I had ended my marriage with my first husband and some boyfriends I had told him about, so he wanted to break up with me before I could break up with him. That statement made no sense to me. Before all the craziness started, I loved him and had no intention of ever leaving him. I'd thought our problems stemmed from his mistaken idea that I didn't like his children. I'd been sure that with time, his feelings about that would change, and our marriage would improve. Now that I knew how dishonest Brad was and knew he was having an affair, everything had changed for me. I didn't believe him when he told me he would come home if I signed a new agreement. If I did sign a new agreement, it would only give him relief and make it easier for him to leave me for Paula. My feeling that the contract renegotiation was another of Brad's setups kept getting stronger and stronger.

Chapter 34

As Brad's affair with Paula became more blatant, our friends didn't approve of how I was being treated, so they helped me any way they could. I would get phone calls telling me he had been seen with her at different places. Brad wasn't liked. His shady business practices and dishonesty were being discovered.

Because good looks were so important to Brad, I couldn't figure out why he would be interested in Paula, who was short and dumpy and wore only dowdy clothes. To me, she was unfeminine, with short hair and unmanicured fingernails. Brad said she had sawed-off short hair and working hands. After seeing her at church one Sunday, he made a comment to me about her short fingers, saying people with short fingers couldn't be trusted.

After Brad fired Jennifer abruptly, she and her husband, Tyler, hated him and became my allies. Since she had worked at the winery for so long, she knew which employees would tell her what Brad was doing, and she would then relay the information to me. Even though she had only worked for three months after Brad bought the winery, she told me she had seen and heard a lot about his bad behavior and womanizing. Martin often visited Brad at the winery, so she got to see firsthand that he wasn't an ethical businessman either and also no angel when it came to women. She even overheard him bragging to someone about his little black book. She also heard Brad tell male employees that everyone should have affairs. Jennifer said she had also overheard employees talking about Brad visiting the house of a woman named Kimberly, who lived nearby. Furthermore, a local woman named Harriet had started riding up to the winery in her horse-drawn carriage. She took Brad for rides through the surrounding wooded area, with the two of them crowded into the small sulky seat. It wasn't long before Jennifer saw him driving a truck pulling Harriet's horse trailer to a race she was competing in.

I had become friends with Donald, a member of our church, who was Harriet's neighbor. He told me about having a dinner party one evening that included Harriet and Brad. Donald said he had been disgusted by Brad's drunken behavior and couldn't see why Harriet would get involved with him. She'd been wearing an expensive bracelet, and when he'd commented on how beautiful it was, she'd said Brad had given it to her and remarked, "That's why I like him." Someone at the party had asked Brad how he and Harriet met, and he'd told them he was at the hardware store, when Harriet walked up to him and just started talking. He'd left and gone to the drugstore, and while he waited for his prescription, Harriet had come in and gotten in line behind him. He'd asked her if she had followed him. She'd told him she was there to get her birth control pills, and he'd told her he was there to get his Viagra. She then had invited him to come to her house for lunch.

Donald told me Harriet had been married three times. The last man she'd been married to had a wealthy mother who'd doled out money to them as she saw fit. To keep from upsetting his mother, he'd stayed married to Harriet until his mother's death. When he'd received his inheritance from his mother's estate, he'd settled with Harriet and left the area, supposedly, according to rumor, to join the LGBTQ community. "To my knowledge, no one ever heard from him again," said Donald.

Jennifer lived almost next door to the winery, so she knew when Brad was there overnight and entertaining women. Paula was still in the picture, calling or visiting Brad every day at the winery. When she was there, Jennifer could see her car on the airplane runway behind the office, where she parked to hide the car from public view. She also had seen Brad drive down to pick her up.

Paula's house wasn't far from the winery, so when Brad spent the night with her, Jennifer could easily see his car parked in her open garage with the back end sticking out. There was a post office just across an open field from Paula's house, and one night, Brad decided to park his car in the post office's parking lot instead of in her garage. Jennifer happened to drive by and notice his car, so she knew he was spending the night with Paula. She was trying to help me get an adultery charge against him, so she called me and told me to come up there. Before leaving the house, I called the local police station to ask if they could do anything to help me. No, they said, adultery wasn't a police matter.

I was so furious with Brad that I wanted to do him serious damage, so I grabbed a can of white spray paint from a basement storage cabinet and took it with me. I met Jennifer and Tyler at a service station near the post office. My Mercedes was easily recognizable, so I rode with them to Brad's car. Hell had no fury like a woman scorned. I got out and spray-painted his car with a few choice words implicating his adultery with Paula and let the air out of his tires.

"Hurry up! Hurry up!" Jennifer kept urging me in a stage whisper. The police station across the street from the post office was making her anxious about getting caught. I hadn't told her I had already tipped off the police.

When I finished, I jumped back into Jennifer's car, panting with excitement. As they drove me back to my car, none of us could stop laughing long enough to say good night to each other. On my drive home, I thought, *Am I having a bad dream or what?*

The next morning, Brad came storming into Riverwood, intent on searching the house for any evidence that I had vandalized his car. I held my breath the whole time because I had put the can of spray paint back in the cabinet. By some miracle, that was the one cabinet he did not open. After he left, I made sure I disposed of the can immediately.

Later that morning, Jennifer called to tell me what was happening at the winery. According to her information, Brad had called the winery to have an air tank brought to him at the post office's parking lot. With air in his tires, he'd driven to the winery and into an equipment garage, where workers had cleaned as much of the paint off the car as they could.

We started laughing all over again about Big Shot Brad driving down the road with those words painted on the side of his car. I told her about his visit to me earlier that morning and how nervous I had been while he was searching the house.

"He did everything he could think of to make me confess," I said. "He even tried to scare me by saying that the car belonged to the corporation instead of him and that I could be in big trouble. I told him it was probably one of Paula's other jealous lovers."

"I'm glad for your sake he didn't find the can," Jennifer said. "There's no telling what he would have done to you if he had. I'll call you if I hear any more news."

Paula became so brazen in her pursuit of Brad that she would even call Riverwood if she thought he might be there and hang up when I answered. She was a member of the vestry of our church. When it became public knowledge that she was sleeping with Brad, another vestry member refused to serve with her and resigned. If any church members still doubted Paula's involvement with Brad, all doubts were taken away one Saturday night when it was her duty to put flowers on the church altar for the Sunday morning church service. When the choir assembled the next morning, they found a note telling them to sing certain "hims." Immediately, most of them knew it had to have been Brad who left the misspelled note, and they let me know he had been with Paula in the church the night before. Her grown children lived in the area, and people soon found out she had been flying off with Brad and lying to her kids about where she was and whom she was with. They thought it was despicable. I had never met anyone as ruthless as Paula. Nothing I or anyone else said to her would get her to stop pursuing Brad. The resigning vestry member told me she had seen Paula and Brad necking in her car parked at a restaurant parking lot. She had also seen them together at a wedding as well as other places. When she asked Paula why she was doing what she was doing, her answer was "He's so much fun."

When I had called Kelton in October and learned without question that Brad was sleeping with Paula, I'd hired a private detective in hopes that an adultery charge would help me with a divorce settlement. He took photos of Brad's car in her open garage and of Paula coming out in a bathrobe and slippers to get the newspaper when Brad's car was there. The private eye reported to me that he was parked in the post office's parking lot one morning, when Paula came racing across the field to him and demanded, "Who are you? Are you watching me?"

When he didn't respond, Paula added, "Just doing your job?"

"Just doing my job," he said.

Brad even had the audacity to tell me that Paula said nice things to him. I replied, "When one is out to break up someone's marriage, I wouldn't expect one to do anything but that."

Early on, Brad and I had looked at houses to buy in the area as an investment and possibly to use as a second home. Brad must have discussed that with Paula, because according to a real estate agent I knew, Paula took him to see a house for sale that was owned by a widow named Rachel. Brad took a liking to Rachel, an attractive blonde, and took her on plane trips, which made Paula furious. Rachel eventually moved to Florida to be with an old man who promised to give her one million dollars when they got married and another million when he died. I thought, *That is a better deal than she would have gotten from Brad.*

"Everyone has a price," Brad had always said.

During all his personal drama, Brad still insisted he would return home if I signed a new contract with him. I still refused, so to hurt me and put pressure on me to do what he wanted me to do, he had me served with a thirty-day eviction notice on March 1 and kept pushing for a divorce, using the previous May as the date we had stopped living together.

I finally admitted to myself that I was in a hopeless marriage. *Oh God, not another divorce.* My life was in shambles. I experienced every emotion possible all at the same time—anger, fear, disgust, sadness, contempt, and even some joy about finally escaping Brad's abuse. I tried my best to come up with an exit plan, but I had many obstacles to overcome. I didn't have a job or anywhere to live. I knew I would be free to move anywhere, but where did I want to go? I was blessed that I had money from the sale of my business and house. I actively tried to come up with answers to those questions.

Chapter 35

MARCH, YEAR SEVEN
RIVERWOOD ESTATE

As time passed, I still didn't know what to do except to keep making plans to leave Riverwood, even though I still had no job and no place to move to. I went back to see the lawyer I had previously seen about the document that gave Martin everything. She was not surprised to see me and readily agreed when I asked her to be my divorce attorney. I gave her the private investigator's report and the photos of Brad's car at Paula's house, but she told me they did not prove adultery. I was devastated.

When the time came for us to give our divorce depositions, Brad's faithful longtime employee Evelyn went to the lawyer's office with the prenuptial document and declared that she had typed it at Riverwood a few days before we were married. All of the pages of the document had been typed on a typewriter, except for the last page, which had been printed out from a computer. It was obvious the last page had been changed. It said that no matter how long Brad and I were married, I wouldn't be entitled to anything. I had heard Brad say many times that when he had been sued over the years, Evelyn had gone to court and said whatever he told her to say, so I knew her testimony wouldn't be truthful.

The reverend who'd married us knew what was in our prenuptial agreement because I had told him about the five-year limit at one of our premarital counseling sessions. I thought his knowing meant I was safe from Brad and Evelyn's untruthfulness. I was sure he could testify that I was telling the truth about the prenup being null and void after five years. However, he told me he couldn't help me because he had also counseled Paula and George during their relationship's ups and downs. I couldn't believe what I was hearing and couldn't understand what that had to do with my agreement with Brad. Reverend Jones gave the reason of confidentiality because of his counseling Paula. Her affair with Brad had been public knowledge for quite some time at that point, so maybe he didn't want to get involved because he knew about Brad's adultery with her. He was the only person who could have helped me.

After we gave our depositions to the attorneys, Brad invited me to go to our favorite restaurant to eat and acted as if nothing had ever happened. He told me I didn't have to leave if I just signed a new contract. I was torn apart. I was on Brad's turf, feeling all alone and confused by his actions toward me. He was telling me I didn't have to go, but he slept with other women and had served me with papers to vacate the property. He told me we could get a divorce and then get remarried. By law, I had to leave Riverwood in thirty days, or the police could come put me and my things out of the house. I didn't trust that Brad would cancel the eviction notice if I agreed to his terms in a new contract.

While all of that was going on, Brad's mother, Vivian, and I became close. She was someone I could call when I was desperate to talk about his actions toward me. She finally told me I needed to leave him. "You could become ill and ruin your health by fooling with him," she said, and she added that a doctor had told Nancy the same thing: her health problems were being caused by Brad. Vivian always gave me accurate information. What Brad didn't share with her himself she would get from Laura by making a friendly call to her and asking what was going on in the business and what Brad was doing in his private life. Laura would readily and honestly tell her grandmother what she knew. I was sure she had no idea Vivian was passing that information on to me.

One evening, when Brad came to Riverwood, we argued,

and he was so angry that he threw some of my clothes into the front yard. After he got into his car and left, I called a neighbor who had become my supporter. She and her husband came over and helped me pick up the clothes and take them to their house for safekeeping. Her husband had helped me before when I was stranded at the house during a bad winter snowstorm and Brad wasn't staying at home. He'd come over and cleared the road from the house to the main road so I could get in and out.

I had to get away from Riverwood. I didn't trust Brad, so I had to be smart about the situation and look after myself. I decided I wanted to be near my friends to have a support system, so I contacted Irene, my real estate friend in Williamsburg, about a place to rent. Then, with the help of my friends, I planned my escape.

I wanted to move without telling Brad so I could take what I needed from the house without interference. Faye came to Riverwood several weekends and helped me pack up boxes and take them to the nearby storage shed I had rented. Jennifer and Tyler came late at night with their van and helped me take larger items to the storage shed. I was careful to leave enough things so the house did not look empty. I did get a scare when Brad came into the house one morning and opened a kitchen cabinet. Luckily, it still had dishes in it. My heart skipped a beat because all of the other cabinets were empty. Another night, it was so late when we finished taking items to the storage shed that at my insistence, Jennifer and Tyler spent the night in our guest room. Jennifer was so uneasy about Brad showing up that they left before daylight the next morning. Jennifer's premonition was right, because Brad arrived at the house soon after they left.

While I was in the process of slowly moving out, Brad and Paula went to Las Vegas and left me at Riverwood with a faulty furnace blowing out black soot. When Jennifer and Tyler came that night to help me, Tyler went to check on the furnace and found an enormous black snake in the basement. It lunged at him when he grabbed it to take it outside. We all thought Brad probably had put the snake there to frighten me.

Chapter 36

MARCH, YEAR SEVEN
RIVERWOOD ESTATE AND
WILLIAMSBURG, VIRGINIA

Vivian let me know that Brad and Rachel were supposed to spend the last week in March at Hatteras together, so that gave me some time to get most of the smaller things I wanted to the storage shed. I prayed they would stay gone until the movers could come get my furniture moved out. I had been unable to find a mover who would move me on the weekend, so it had to be on Monday morning. I had warned the moving company about my volatile circumstances and the possibility of trouble.

My concern about moving out unmolested started when one of Brad's employees came to the house to mow the lawn. I asked him not to tell Brad I was moving out. What did the employee do? He called Brad and tipped him off. Unfortunately, Brad had already returned from his trip. When Jennifer received word from her spy inside the company that Brad was on his way to Riverwood, she called to warn me. I called 911 and asked for help. When the officer arrived, he told me that there was nothing he could do and that the lawyers would have to work it out.

Brad's car soon came speeding down the road toward the house, where a big moving truck was backed up to the front steps. A few pieces of furniture were already loaded onto the truck. He told the movers they were robbing him and were going to jail. He was so threatening that they called their boss, who told them to come back to the office with the furniture that was already in the truck. Brad got our lawyers involved, and they agreed for us to meet at the mover's storage facility the next morning so Brad could sort through the furniture and get what he considered to be his. While the lawyers worked out the situation, Brad tried to intimidate me further by calling for backup from Martin and Regan Miller, the company CPA, who came speeding up to the house, jumped out of their cars, and took seats on the front porch.

I was so disheartened by everything that had happened that I went upstairs and lay down on a mattress, the only thing left in the bedroom. Brad followed me upstairs, lay down beside me, held me in his arms, and told me again that I didn't have to leave. I thought to myself, *You must be kidding. Do you really expect me to trust you?* My reply to him was "You have had the best, and now you must settle for less."

After all the trauma I had experienced that day, I was so disgusted I decided I wasn't going to go to the mover's storage area the next morning. *Brad can have it all—I'm leaving Riverwood at the first sign of daylight.*

Chapter 37

APRIL TO JULY, YEAR SEVEN
WILLIAMSBURG, VIRGINIA

When I left in the wee hours of the morning on April 1, only Jennifer and Tyler knew what I was doing. They met me at a nearby restaurant and insisted on loading their van with items from my storage area so they could follow me to Williamsburg and help me get checked into my new home.

When we got to the rental office, Irene gave me the key to the house I had rented sight unseen. When she had told me about the house, I'd asked her if she would live there. She'd said yes, so I'd told her to rent the house for me and sent her a deposit. She had encouraged me to move back to Williamsburg because she had a business in mind for me to buy. She went to Robbie, the same hairdresser I had gone to when I lived there, and he had recently told her he was tired of doing paperwork and wanted to sell his business. She thought I could buy his salon and put an accessory boutique in the front part of the shop.

At the rental house, we unloaded our vehicles, and then we went out for a late dinner and settled in for the night. Since there was no furniture, we had to sleep on the floor. The next morning, Jennifer and Tyler went with me to buy a new mattress set, sheets, and a few other things I needed before they left to go back to their home.

In the meantime, Brad was aggressively trying to locate me.

He called everyone he could think of to ask if anyone knew where I might be. The few people who did know, such as Irene and Faye, wouldn't tell him. Unfortunately, I had to give my new address to my lawyer so she could send me papers to sign. Since Brad's lawyer was privy to the papers, which included my address, it wasn't long before Brad knew my location and called me. *So much for hiding*, I thought. I didn't welcome his call.

Next, a counselor called me on Brad's behalf. I was still raging angry and told her to tell Brad he needed to learn how to treat a woman and not physically hurt her. That was the last I heard from her, but it didn't halt Brad's quest to get me back.

During the month of April, Jennifer and Tyler helped me move the remaining items from the storage shed, and I also retrieved the boxes friends had been keeping for me. I eventually got a call from the movers to arrange for delivery of the items Brad had not kept. The next time I met with my attorney, she showed me photos she had taken of Brad and Laura going through the furniture. Laura again had to hold her dad's hand to keep her high-paying job with benefits secure.

After I had spent time investigating the business Irene had in mind for me to buy, the deal fell through, so I still didn't have anything worked out about a job, and that was another frightening thing to have to deal with, especially since I had just signed a year's lease on my rental house. Irene introduced me to a business broker she knew. After searching through his many listings, I came across a custom drapery shop that sounded similar to my interior design shop. Most importantly, it was a business I could afford to buy. I visited the drapery shop and even worked there for a few days before deciding to put down a deposit to make the business my own. It met all my needs and was an established money-maker. I needed income to live on right away. I didn't have time to start and nurture a business for years before taking a salary. There was another potential buyer who desperately wanted the business. He was so upset when I outbid him that he pleaded with me to sell it to him.

After agreeing to buy the shop, I had my work cut out for me for the next couple months with getting insurance, incorporating the business, setting up a credit line with vendors and the building owner, having the utilities switched over to my name, getting a tax ID number, and interviewing the current employees. On and on it went. Buying an established business or starting a new business was overwhelming.

Brad began showing up at my home unannounced. He kept asking me how I had arranged to do so much. Who had helped me? I remained smug about my moving accomplishment and wouldn't tell him anything about how I had managed to remove items without his knowing about it. When he learned of my plan to buy the drapery shop, he turned on the charm, telling me I could move back to Riverwood and take the guesthouse to use for my office. He also begged me to let the other bidder have the shop so I could move back to Riverwood, but my goal was to be self-sufficient, safe, and free of abuse.

I closed on the business Friday afternoon, July 1. Since it was a holiday weekend, the business was closed until July 5. Part of my buyer's agreement was that the previous owner would stay on through the month of July as a training period for me. Brad had made big plans for us to celebrate the Fourth of July together, so we went to Wilmington so he could enjoy swimming in the ocean. It turned out to be a pleasant weekend. My mother was out of town, so we had her house all to ourselves. The next weekend, when I had my grand opening, Brad sent me a dozen red roses and a note of congratulations.

By then, my feelings for Brad were changing from being in love with him to having an ulterior motive for continuing our relationship. Since I wasn't getting alimony from him, I knew I could use his financial help to establish my new business. Brad was in a position to help me so that I could use less of my savings, so I encouraged his continued interest in me.

Chapter 38

JULY TO OCTOBER, YEAR SEVEN
WILLIAMSBURG, VIRGINIA

A lot had happened in my life in the four months since I had left Riverwood, but I still had to make trips to Charlottesville for meetings with Brad and our two lawyers. We had been married for more than five years, so our prenup was invalid, but I didn't have a copy of it. My attorney was desperately trying to work out a decent settlement with Brad and his lawyer. By that time, Brad was making regular visits to see me in Williamsburg and had started inviting me to go with him to weekend events he was planning to attend.

Every time we completed a meeting with our lawyers, Brad would ask me to go to the nearby Ruth Chris Steak House with him. He behaved as if nothing out of the ordinary had just happened. He even tried to stay on my good side by coming to the hotel room where I was staying. On the other hand, he was using his usual tactic: wear people out and cost them so much money that they'll just throw up their hands and forget the suit against him. He was always asking for some paper from my attorney, knowing I would incur a charge for him to get the information for his lawyer. I was even beginning to believe my attorney was working on Brad's side because of the "short-term marriage" comments she made to me. She considered a six-year marriage short-term.

Finally, Brad and both lawyers agreed to offer me a portion of the back pay he had promised me that I had never received as my divorce settlement. I still had to pay my lawyer. I knew that continuing to deal with them was a waste of my time and energy, so I agreed to take the offer. My business was doing well, and I no longer needed anything Brad had. God had answered my prayers.

Brad was still trying to talk me into selling my business and moving back to Riverwood. He continued coming to Williamsburg on Wednesday evenings and weekends to take me out for dinner and dancing. He was still jealous of me. One night at the restaurant, Bob, an advertising account executive I had met while getting my business advertising set up with the local paper, was there also. We recognized each other, and he came over and gave me a huge hug. Bob was tall and good looking, and the greeting he gave me was enough to cause Brad to take me by the arm and leave the restaurant. Even though we were legally separated, he demanded I explain how I knew Bob and why he had hugged me like that.

Another man who had helped me with advertising came by my house one day when Brad was there. Brad answered the door, said something ugly to him, and closed the door in his face. When the man immediately knocked again, I dashed to the door ahead of Brad to assure my friend I was all right before Brad shoved past me, told him to get out of there, and slammed the door.

One Sunday, when I arrived back home from a weekend at Riverwood, I found divorce papers in my mailbox. When I called Brad and told him, he said I should have been expecting them. I'd always thought people had to live separately without any sexual relations for six months to qualify for getting a divorce in the state of Virginia. As far as I was concerned, Brad had obtained an illegal divorce from me. When I told my lawyer, she said, "You could go before the judge and contest the divorce," but I decided I had better things to do with my time. Again, rules and laws were made for other people, not for Brad.

Once all of Brad's attempts to renegotiate our marital contract had failed and we were officially divorced, his goal was for us to remarry. The divorce had relieved him from our initial contract, and I would be forced to agree to different terms if we remarried.

Chapter 39

The subdivision in Williamsburg where I was renting a house wasn't the best area in town. Brad kept telling me I needed to buy another house in the Kingsmill gated community. Although the lease on the house I was renting wouldn't be up for several months, I started house hunting and found a house not far from my old house in Kingsmill that I liked very much, and I bought it. I started making a few improvements on the house that I wanted to finish before I moved in. Brad even had some workmen he knew come do some of the repairs. When my moving day finally arrived, Brad and some of his employees moved me from the rental house into my Kingsmill house.

Martha contacted me soon after I moved into my house. She had married a military officer a few years back, and he had just gotten orders to be transferred to Florida. She was worried about what was going to happen to the interior design shop she'd bought from me, and she asked if I would be willing to buy it back. Since the drapery business I owned could be merged with the design shop into one big, profitable enterprise, I jumped at the opportunity. Brad helped by going with me to buy supplies and repairing equipment for me. He even got his CPA to keep my books.

To my surprise, one afternoon, Brad drove up to my house with a brand-new boat on a trailer so we would have a boat in

Williamsburg. I found the boat to be a nice way to relax on weekends and get away from my business responsibilities for a while. I wasn't a fisherman, so I was able to catch up on my reading while Brad fished in the York River.

Brad had his copilot fly down to Wilmington and bring my mother to Williamsburg so she could see my newly remodeled home. He was still doing nice things for me, such as flying me to and from Riverwood on some weekends. He also let me drive his newly leased red convertible Jaguar back and forth to Riverwood and use it during the week, telling me that if I came back, he would buy me a new Jag. It wasn't long before he told me I had to give the car back because he said I was putting too many miles on it. I didn't think a red convertible suited his personality, so I assumed he'd leased it to attract the attention of women and show off while dating. I had never known him to drive anything but a full-size luxury Cadillac.

I had barely gotten settled into my new house before Brad started encouraging me to purchase a larger, more expensive home. I wouldn't bite because I knew his game of getting control of people by helping them get in over their heads.

Chapter 40

YEARS EIGHT AND NINE
RIVERWOOD ESTATE AND
WILLIAMSBURG, VIRGINIA

Over the next two years, Brad and I continued to visit each other; I went to Riverwood on weekends, and he came to Williamsburg on Wednesdays. We went on a few trips and even took ballroom dancing lessons. He was helpful to me, but I still found evidence of his involvement with Paula and other women when I visited Riverwood. He didn't enjoy coming to Williamsburg because of the heavy traffic and couldn't understand why I wanted to live there instead of on a beautiful country estate. "Because," I told him in exasperation, "my friends helped me move and get established back in this area. They would think I was crazy if I went back to Riverwood." The standoff persisted.

Brad still wanted us to remarry and continued his unrelenting request that I sell my business, move back to Riverwood, and use the guesthouse for my office if I still wanted to have a business. When we'd first met, he had been crafty enough to know what would hook me and lead me to abandon my life for him. I now believed he saw me as the means to hone his rough edges, so to speak, and be accepted by the power people and envied by other men for having a beautiful wife. He knew from my experience with Ray that I would be an excellent hostess and would use my designer experience to make his house a showcase for the influential people he desired to cultivate. It was obvious he wanted a good woman to keep the home fires burning, but I realized he also wanted the freedom and excitement of seeing other women. I refused to let him lure me into his craziness again. I would not entertain the thought of remarrying him, because I still found voice messages from women on his answering machine when I visited him. I felt if Brad truly had wanted our relationship to work, he would have left other women alone.

That summer, we began seeing yet another counselor. When I told her how upset I got when women called him while I was at Riverwood, she responded, "Just don't go there." I lost faith in her after that remark. I didn't understand why Brad would want me to go to counseling with him if he was not going to change his ways.

I felt I would never be able to trust him to the point that I would be willing to give up my business and home for him again. Having him as a friend to do things with was okay, but I was so busy running my large business and taking care of my home that I wasn't interested in remarrying him or even in finding a new person to start a relationship with. I thought Brad was beginning to figure that out, because in the two years since our divorce, he had made no headway in any of his requests, and my independent side was stronger than ever. I had disappointed Brad by being able to take care of myself. When he'd had me evicted, he'd told me I would end up in my mother's back bedroom. He'd thought he would make me destitute so he could easily gain control of me and bully me.

My mother passed away unexpectedly the week before Thanksgiving that year. Brad flew me to Wilmington but didn't stay for the funeral. That hurt my feelings. He did come back to Wilmington to fly me back home, but unbelievably, he asked me to pay him for the two trips. When the plane landed, he said, "Call me when you get over this."

I spent that Christmas at home alone, except for a few phone calls from family members wishing me a merry Christmas. It gave me a lot of time to think about the slow final ending of my love for Brad. Over time, bit by bit, my love for him had faded. I could tell the end of even our friendship was near—I felt no love for him, and I no longer even cared that he was seeing other women. I met people at work who invited me to do things, and I was even starting to have small parties at my home. I had developed a social life that didn't include Brad.

Needless to say, Brad didn't get a call from me during the holidays, and he didn't call me either. Sometime in January, he called and acted as if nothing were wrong between us. He asked me if I would go with him to have a medical procedure done. "No," I replied. "Have one of the women you see go with you." His daughter ended up going with him.

Brad continued to visit me occasionally early in the new year and invited me on a few trips. On one trip, we spent a few days with Martin and Addison in a vacation house they had rented on Sanibel Island, Florida. Another time, he asked me to help him with a party at Riverwood. Unbeknownst to me, he had put Laura in charge, and she was not happy about any suggestion I made. I thought she acted peeved about having to help Brad with a party in the first place. I quickly made the decision to withdraw and took a seat on the side porch with other guests. Riverwood no longer felt like home to me, particularly since Ida Mae had passed away.

Brad asked me again two more times that year what it would take for me to go back. Finally, the answer flew out of my mouth, and I surprised even myself: "You don't have enough!" I at last knew for sure my feelings for Brad had totally changed. I was finally over the hurt he had caused me, and the love I'd had for him had been destroyed.

After that, Brad finally gave up on getting me back. His mother told me he went around asking all the single women he knew if they would marry him. Paula said no. Margot, a woman he had seen in Richmond, initially declined and then later changed her mind and said yes, but lucky for her, Harriet had already accepted Brad's marriage proposal. Harriet must have felt special and loved to be the fourth woman Brad proposed to within a few days. *I guess when a woman is desperate for a man, she looks the other way when the man has sex with other women*, I thought. I was not willing to settle for that kind of relationship. I hadn't known about Brad's bad reputation when I first became involved with him because I hadn't lived in his area or known any of the people who knew him. Those women lived in the area and knew his bad reputation, and they still went after him. Even his mother said she didn't know what any woman would want with him. I knew they wanted only his money, certainly not him!

Not long after Brad and Harriet's quick wedding, he came to me and asked for a sexual favor. I briefly considered doing it for revenge on Harriet but couldn't bring myself to stoop that low. He told me the sex had been great when he and Harriet first got married, but it wasn't anymore. *Yeah*, I thought. *That's probably the same line you used when you were out committing adultery when we were married. Christina, count your blessings that you're through with him.*

During that visit, Brad told me he was having business difficulties. Martin had been in drug rehab twice, and he and Addison were getting a divorce because of his infidelity. *Proving*, I thought, *apples don't fall far from the tree.*

Brad went on. "Martin's drug use and reckless spending made him lose the business I gave him, and now he's under investigation for bid rigging, so he might even go to jail. He can't find a job because he has such a bad reputation, so I put him to work at the winery. That's a hardship for me because the winery isn't as profitable as I thought it would be."

Huh, I thought. *Serves you right.*

That visit ended our relationship on all levels. Brad was out of my life for good. When I thought about it later, I realized that when he'd asked what it would take for me to return to Riverwood, I had failed to tell him the real answer: his love and faithfulness were all I'd wanted from him. My life with him had revolved around his money. The life of luxury I had enjoyed as the wife of a wealthy man had caused me to forget my knowledge of the important things that made a good relationship. I now knew for sure I had made the right decision not to remarry Brad and return to Riverwood.

Chapter 41

About a year after my last contact with Brad, I was unwinding from my busy workday with a glass of wine and the newspaper. As I turned the page, I saw the headline "Indicted Exec of Construction Firm Dies in Plane Crash." As I began reading the article, I quickly realized the man was my ex-husband, Brad. *He's dead!* I composed myself enough to continue reading the article, which said,

> Bradford Hightower was killed in a fiery twin-engine airplane crash on Tuesday, a day after receiving an indictment from a federal grand jury for conspiring to rig bids to buy leases in Virginia. He was the only occupant in the Baron aircraft when it slammed into the side of Afton Mountain near Charlottesville shortly after six o'clock in the morning. Police say it is too early to tell if the collision was intentional. Hightower was suspected of orchestrating a scheme between two large construction companies for many years, said the Department of Justice in a released statement. The companies decided ahead of time who would win bids, with

the winner allocating an interest in the leases to the other company. On Monday, Hightower released a statement denying the charges. "The charges that have been filed against me today are wrong and unprecedented," Hightower said. "Anyone who knows me, my business record, and the industry in which I have worked for many years knows that I could not be guilty of violating any laws."

Printed in the United States
By Bookmasters